# If You Really
# L♥VED ME

ANNE SCHRAFF

# URBAN UNDERGROUND

A Boy Called Twister

The Fairest

**If You Really Loved Me**

Like a Broken Doll

One of Us

Outrunning the Darkness

The Quality of Mercy

Shadows of Guilt

To Be a Man

Wildflower

SADDLEBACK
EDUCATIONAL PUBLISHING
www.sdlback.com

ISBN-13: 978-1-61651-003-9
ISBN-10: 1-61651-003-X
eBook: 978-1-60291-788-0

Printed in Guangzhou, China
0510/05-72-10

15 14 13 12 11   2 3 4 5

# CHAPTER ONE

Destini Fletcher shut off the alarm and turned onto her side. She wasn't going to school today. Or maybe ever again. She snuggled deeper under the blankets and tried to recover the wonderful sleep that the shrill alarm had taken from her.

"Destini!" Her mother's voice—almost as shrill as the alarm—came at her. "Are you up yet, girl?"

"I'm sick, Mom," Destini wailed. "I can't go to school today."

Mom appeared in the doorway of the bedroom like an angry witch. "Destini Fletcher," Mom yelled, "you are no more sick than I am. Get your lazy body out of that bed and take your shower and get

1

moving. I am sick and tired of having this fight most every day."

"Mom, my head hurts and my stomach hurts and—" Destini began reciting her ailments, but her mother came over to the bed and ripped off her blanket.

"Nothing hurts and you know it," Mom scolded. "You just don't like school and you think it's okay to skip going just because you have a fancy to. You are just like your no-good father who never would go to work because he just didn't like working. Well, I'm not letting my only child go down the drain because she has her father's lazy genes. You are getting out of bed and into the shower if I have to drag you by your hair, girl."

Destini dropped her legs over the side of the bed. "Nothing ever goes on at that stupid school anyway," she whined. "We have really crummy teachers, and everything we learn is stupid and boring. I'm not learning anything I can use. I mean, who cares why some old men who've been dead for two hundred years wrote some dumb laws?"

"Other kids are learning and getting good grades, and getting set for college and making something of themselves, girl," Mom chided. " You are sixteen years old. You're not some day care baby. You got to have some responsibility. School is what you make it. All you want to do is watch TV or play on the computer looking for pictures of boys. You are boy crazy, Destini."

Destini laughed bitterly. "I don't even have a boyfriend. That's a big laugh, Mom. I don't have a boyfriend. I never had a boyfriend. Every other junior has a boyfriend, but the boys won't look at me because I dress so awful in such old-fashioned clothes," Destini complained, walking toward the bathroom. Destini was saving up to buy the newer styles, but in the meantime she was stuck with what was in her closet.

"You don't look no worse than most of the other girls except those who dress trashy—which I won't allow," Mom asserted. "Now get your shower done and get dressed. You got to eat breakfast and catch the bus to school."

Destini hated Harriet Tubman High School from the moment she started as a freshman. She was not as pretty or as smart as the other girls. That's what she thought anyway. Now that she was a junior, things were worse. Now it seemed that *all* the girls were cuter than she was. There was a girl in American history named Sereeta Prince who was so beautiful she looked like a model. Sometimes Destini felt like slapping Sereeta in the face because she was so pretty and because she had a handsome boyfriend. But, of course, it wasn't Sereeta's fault.

After her shower, Destini walked leadenly toward the breakfast table. Her hair was still wet. She tugged at it bitterly. "Look!" she exclaimed. "It's all frizzy and horrible. I look like some clown or something. I hate my hair. I wish I could get it straightened or something. I know girls who do that."

4

"Nothin' wrong with your hair, girl. It's perfectly all right," Mom assured her. "You don't need to change what you got. What's wrong with you, girl?"

Destini looked at the scrambled eggs and the little brown sausages. "I hate eggs and sausage," she complained. "They make you fat. I'm already too fat."

"You are not in the least bit fat," Mom said, busy around the table. "You weigh just what you're supposed to, Destini. Now eat your breakfast and stop givin' me grief. I'm tellin' you, girl, if I'd known the kind of grief you were going to cause me, I woulda sent you down to the county home to raise you when you were a baby."

Destini picked at her food, finishing only her orange juice. She nibbled on a bran muffin, ate half a sausage, and then got up from the table. "The stupid bus will be at the corner in a minute," Destini grumbled. "If I miss it I gotta wait for the next one. Our stupid old school doesn't even have a school bus. We gotta ride the stinky city bus, and the drivers hate us kids when we get on with our backpacks."

Destini walked down to the corner of Seminole Street to the bus stop. Already some kids were waiting there. They were not her friends, but they were in some of her classes. Destini did not make friends easily. She thought most of the kids at Tubman High were better off than she was. To her, either their families had more money or they were more attractive or popular. Some of the parents had good jobs, but Destini's mother was a housekeeper at the local hospital. All day she pushed carts filled with dirty laundry in blue bags. Some of the kids had parents who were teachers or nurses. Their homes were nicer too. And Destini hated the cramped little two-bedroom duplex where she lived with Mom.

A girl named Carissa Polson got on the bus at the next stop. She saw Destini and smiled. "Hi," she nodded.

"Hi," Destini replied. Carissa was pretty too. Her mother didn't work but her father was in sales. Several boys wanted to date Carissa, but she settled on a good-looking athlete on the track team, Kevin Walker.

"Are you ready for the test in English?" Carissa asked Destini from the seat behind her. Destini supposed Carissa was all right. She was nice enough, but Destini was jealous of her. She was too pretty and her boyfriend was too cute. "No," Destini replied, "I never learn anything in English. Mr. Pippin is a terrible teacher. I don't know what those stories we have to read are all about."

Two boys got on the bus at the next stop. Destini thought one of them was really good-looking. He had broad shoulders and a nice face. There was an empty seat next to Destini. She slid closer to the window and pulled her backpack under her feet to make room. But the boy was looking at Carissa. Even though he had to sit with his feet in the aisle, he sat next to Carissa. "Hi Carissa," he said warmly.

Destini took a long, deep breath. "It isn't fair," she thought. "Why do some girls look so cute, and why do I look so plain?" It's not that Destiny was awful looking or anything, but she just wasn't pretty in the way Sereeta and Carissa were. Boys looked at her as if she was a dull brown gingerbread cake and all around her were lemon meringue pies and strawberry shortcakes. The boys would glance at her and then go on to something tastier looking.

The boy with the broad shoulders was trying to engage Carissa in conversation, but Carissa wasn't saying much. She already had a great boyfriend. She didn't need this boy's attention.

"Not fair!" Destini thought again. Carissa did not need this boy fawning over her. She wasn't interested in him. Why didn't he come and sit by Destini, who made room for him and who would have loved to talk to him? It would have made her morning if he had just sat next to her and exchanged a few words. But, no, there he was bothering Carissa who didn't want or need him.

Tubman High loomed in the bus window and Destini sighed deeply again. She hoisted her backpack onto her shoulders and headed for the door. Students were passing by the statue of Harriet Tubman, for whom the school was named. When Destini first came here, she stopped and took a good look at the statue of Tubman. She had such a plain face. Actually, she was homely. She did many wonderful things, leading black men, women, and children out of brutal slavery and into freedom in Canada. She was a good and brave and wonderful woman, but men did not like her either.

Destini felt a kinship with Harriet Tubman. Her husband had left her for a prettier woman—it was said—but she didn't care. Destini thought she probably *did* care but she was too proud to say so. Destini read a biography of Tubman, who said of her husband who left her that he had dropped right out of her heart. She said if he could live without her, then she could live without him. And so she did.

Destini wished she could feel that way about the boys at Tubman High. If they didn't want her, then, fine, she could do without them too. But she wanted a boyfriend. She wanted to go on dates, as Carissa and Sereeta did. She wanted to walk, hands linked, across the campus with a boy.

It just wasn't fair.

Destini went into English. Mr. Pippin was handing out the quizzes, and Destini took hers without much hope. Mom kept telling her if she didn't study she couldn't make decent grades and couldn't go to college. Mom warned her that if she didn't buckle down, she would end up in a hospital pushing carts filled with dirty laundry in blue bags.

"Don't you depend on some man coming along and putting your life in order girl," Mom often preached. "There ain't no Prince Charmings anymore, if there ever was any. Them days are gone forever. Men don't take care of their women no more. The woman has to go and work as hard as the man does, and on top of that she's got to bear the children and take care of them. And most likely the man is gonna get tired of you someday and dump you like an old shoe. Or he's gonna be some no-account that you got to throw him out like I did with your father. He never took care of us. All he did was eat here. Now it's all on me. My legs ache and my back hurts, but I got to keep movin' 'cause I got no decent education. It could be different for you. Your future is in your own hands. I'm scrimpin' and scrapin' for your college fund, so you can have a good job, a decent future."

Destini read the questions on the quiz. They might as well have been written in Greek. She couldn't match the stories with their authors. She guessed at everything. After Mr. Pippin picked up the answer sheets, he had a brief discussion of a new story.

"This is by H. G. Wells," he said. " 'The Door in the Wall.' "

There was a disturbance in the back row. A tall boy was swatting at something. "A fly's buzzin' around me," the boy said.

"There are no flies in here," Mr. Pippin said.

"Yeah, it's buzzing," insisted the boy— Marko Lane. He was swatting at it with his jacket. Everybody started laughing, and two other boys joined in the uproar. Destini had to laugh too. Mr. Pippin grew so agitated that he was waving his arms in the air, demanding quiet. It was one of the funniest things Destini had ever seen. Mr. Pippin was flushed and breathing heavily when order was finally restored. During the commotion, a boy made eye contact with Destini. He was a nice looking boy. A bit overweight, his midsection had the start of a spare tire. When he looked at Destini he smiled and she smiled back. For just a second they connected, sharing the amusement at the invisible mosquito and Mr. Pippin.

After class, as everybody was leaving, the boy came alongside Destini and asked, "Hey, wasn't that hilarious? That was funnier than most movies. Marko really knows how to stir things up in that creepy class."

CHAPTER ONE

"Yeah, it was a scream," Destini agreed. "I laughed so hard I got tears in my eyes. I hate that class."

"Me too. Hey, I'm Tyron Becker. You're Destini, right?" he said.

"Yes," Destini replied, growing weak.

"I've seen you in a couple of my classes," he said he went on.

"I've seen you too," Destini responded. She felt strange. Is this how it all starts? Suddenly, out of nowhere a boy comes along and shows some interest. Just a tiny, flickering flame. Then, little by little, it grows.

"Well, see you around, Destini," Tyron said, smiling again. He seemed to look right into her eyes. Boys didn't usually do that. They looked around her, through her, beyond her. But Tyron's gaze lingered as if he found something engaging in Destini's face.

Destini was excited. She walked to the snack machine, fantasizing. Maybe she'd end up with a boyfriend. She was not expecting any big deal, just a boy she might hang out with at lunch sometimes. Just a boy she could be around while the other girls giggled and stood close to their boyfriends.

Destini bought an apple. Usually she got something sweet, but she didn't want to gain weight. She weighed only a hundred and twenty on her five-foot-four frame, but some of the other girls—the popular ones—were way thinner and the boys seemed to like that.

All during her next class, American History I with Ms. McDowell, Destini thought about Tyron. Tyron usually hung with Marko Lane, who had a beautiful girlfriend named Jasmine. Her hair was reddish and gorgeous, not frizzy like Destini's. Tyron and his friends were always in the thick of things, and Destini longed to be part of that.

"So what was President Carter's priority in the Iran hostage crisis," Ms. McDowell asked. "Destini?"

Destini had neither read the chapter nor listened to the lecture. "He, uh . . . wanted to get the fighting stopped," Destini mumbled.

"What fighting?" Ms. McDowell asked.

"Uh . . . the Iranians," Destini stammered. "They were fighting us, right? And soldiers were getting killed and stuff?" Destini felt like an idiot. The students around her were smirking.

"Destini, would you see me after class?" Ms. McDowell requested before proceeding. Torie McDowell was a very beautiful woman and probably one of the best history teachers in the district. She was in her early thirties and looked even younger, when she was walking around town in her jeans and tank tops. More than a few boys in the class had crushes on her, but she was totally professional.

When everybody had left, Ms. McDowell directed, "Please take a seat up front here, Destini."

"Yes ma'am," Destini said nervously.

"Destini, you didn't have a clue about the Iran hostage crisis we've been talking about. Obviously you didn't read about it or listen to the class discussion," Ms. McDowell began. "You are an intelligent girl, and I hate to see your grades going down because you put no effort in. You got a D in your last test."

"I'm sorry, Ms. McDowell, I'll try to do better," Destini responded.

"Are there any problems that I might help you with? Do you have a good place to study at home or are there a lot of distractions?" the teacher asked.

"No, that's all okay," Destini replied, finally raising her eyes and looking at the teacher. Ms. McDowell seemed to really care. She was young enough to remember what it was like to be Destini's age. She was probably even dating now. She must know how important it is for a girl to have a social life. Destini decided to say something. "See, Ms. McDowell, I feel really lonely at school."

"Lonely?" Ms. McDowell repeated. "Have you thought about joining one of the clubs?"

"No," Destini explained, "I mean, I've never had a boyfriend. I mean, well, you're very pretty, Ms. McDowell, so I bet you had a lot of boyfriends when you were in high school. But I never did have one and I'm sixteen years old and all the other girls have boyfriends." Destini was ashamed for even bringing up her feelings. She feared the teacher would think she was an idiot or something.

"Destini, sixteen is very, *very* young," Ms. McDowell responded. "A lot of girls don't have boyfriends at your age. You just focus on the girls who do, but you don't even notice how many don't have boyfriends. I didn't have a boyfriend at all in high school. I didn't date until I got to college. Boyfriends were not my priority. I wanted to get a good education. I wanted to be somebody—a teacher. I was busy making a good life for myself."

"Yeah, that's what my mom is always telling me, but I . . . just wish I had a guy who sorta liked me," Destini confided.

"Believe me, Destini," Ms. McDowell assured her, "there'll be plenty of time for boyfriends, but if you blow your shot at a good education, the opportunity may never come again. You are a very lovely young woman. You have no need to worry about boyfriends in your future, but right now get a good education. Okay?"

"Okay," Destini agreed. But in her heart all she could think of was how Tyron Becker smiled at her.

# CHAPTER TWO

Later in the day, as Destini was walking to the school library, she spotted Tyron walking alone. Her heart raced. Would he acknowledge her? Was their budding friendship far enough along that he might smile or nod when their paths crossed?

Destini deliberately changed course so that they would meet. He could not miss her. She thought that if he completely ignored her, she might die. But as they neared each other, Tyron called out, "Hi Destini! How's it going?"

"Pretty good," Destini called back. "Just one more class."

"Yeah, hooray!" he cried. "Then we're outta here." He was still smiling. He was looking at her. He wasn't acting like most boys, as if she were an insect to be stepped over.

Waiting for the bus to take her home, Destini was unreasonably cheered. She was not nearly as bitter as she had been this morning. Usually her mother did not get home until around seven and then started dinner. And usually Destini did not do much to help her. "Tonight will be different," Destini thought. She felt upbeat. She would surprise Mom by cutting up the salad and boiling the pasta. When Mom got home, almost everything would be ready. All Mom would need to do is add the cooked shrimp in the refrigerator and the dressing.

At home, Destini went to her room, then sat down with the Tubman High yearbook from last year. You could consult the index to find where each student was pictured. Every year the seniors got big, full-color photos, but the underclass kids were photographed too. The athletes had many photos, but Destini was lucky to get her one dismal little sophomore photo. Destini hated the picture. She looked even plainer and stupider than she really was. But Destini was not interested in her own photo. She was looking for pictures of Tyron.

Tyron looked nice in his photo. He was smiling and looking almost handsome. He also played football, so there were some great action photos of him. One showed him hurling the football and he looked great. Destini looked at the pictures of Tyron, over and over again. She wondered what was ahead.

Would he have looked into her eyes so steadily and smiled if he wasn't at least a little bit interested?

Destini walked over to her bedroom mirror and tried to smooth down her frizzy hair. She went to her mom's room and used some of her hair spray. That seemed to help a little. Then Destini went back to her closet to search for something nice to wear tomorrow. Destini liked red, so she picked a red sweater that fit her snugly. She found her best pair of jeans, the ones that showed off her figure. Then Destini realized Mom would be home soon, and she hurried to the kitchen to start the dinner and set the table.

"Hi Mom!" Destini greeted her mother as she came in.

"What on earth!" Mom cried out. "I have died and gone to heaven! Hallelujah! Dinner is ready and the table is set. Child, what is going on? Have you lost your mind?"

"Mommm," Destini giggled. "I just wanted to do something nice for you 'cause I've been giving you a hard time. I know I can be a pain in the behind."

"Destini, baby," Mom said, "this is just so nice. I am very tired tonight and I was dreading fixing dinner."

"Well, I had a good day, Mom," Destini announced. "My history teacher, Ms. McDowell, she was really nice. She told me I'm smart but I need to study more and I'm going to. I'm going to read the whole chapter she assigned tonight" Destini did not tell her mother the real reason she was so elated. Mom would not be thrilled. She was very leery of men and boys.

After dinner, Destini called Alonee Lennox. Destini had no close girlfriends at Tubman, but once in a while she talked to Alonee.

"Whatcha doing, Alonee?" she asked.

"Reading 'The String' for English," Alonee replied.

"I made dinner for my mom. She was really thrilled," Destini told Alonee. "Mom works so hard."

"Good for you," Alonee encouraged her.

"Alonee," Destini went on, "reason I called . . . some guy from school was kinda giving me the once-over. He was smiling at me and stuff, and I think maybe he wants to be friends or something. Do you know Tyron Becker?"

Alonee said nothing for a second or two, then she said in a cautious voice, "I don't know him really well, but he's close with Marko Lane. Marko is one of the jokers who mess up a lot of classes. I'm not real crazy about him."

"Yeah," Destini agreed. "He was messing around in English today, huh?"

"The fly thing. Poor Mr. Pippin," Alonee said.

"I was wondering," Destini probed, "I suppose Tyron has a girlfriend . . . "

"No, I've never seen him steady with anybody," Alonee answered. "He doesn't seem to have a big social life."

"That makes two of us, huh? I mean Tyron and me," Destini asked. "Well, anyways, I guess I better go to bed and get my beauty sleep. Night, Alonee."

Destini flopped into bed and hugged her pillow. Tyron didn't have a girlfriend! She kept playing that fact over and over in her mind.

*He didn't have a girlfriend. Not a steady one.*

Destini couldn't go to sleep. She lay there dreaming. She wondered what kind of music Tyron liked. What kind of food did he like—burgers, pizza, chicken? Tyron didn't dress well, at least not as well as Marko did. Marko always looked great. But sometimes it looked like Tyron was wearing some of Marko's old clothes. They didn't fit just right. Marko was leaner than Tyron and the clothing looked tight on Tyron. Thinking about that made Destini a little sad. Poor Tyron. He wanted to wear great clothes, but his family couldn't afford them. Destini read her history assignment and finally went to sleep, dreaming about Tyron.

Getting out of bed for school the next morning was no problem for Destini. She showered and used the new body wash that smelled of vanilla. Then she slipped on her red sweater and the jeans. She came to the kitchen to eat breakfast in a happy mood.

"Well, it's good to see you smiling in the morning, girl," Mom greeted.

"Yeah Mom, I've just decided to have a better attitude," Destini declared.

"Oh, I heard from your father yester-day," Mom reported. "He'd been at the racetrack again and lo and behold he won for a change. The big spender handed me a coupla hundred dollars. He told me to give you a twenty so you can buy some-thing nice."

Destini took the twenty dollar bill and asked, "Did he want to know how I was doing in school?"

"He was kinda drunk, baby," Mom de-clared sadly. "He wasn't making much sense. Now, when he gets sober, he'll remember he gave away all that money he won on the ponies and he'll come around wanting it back, but he'll be barking up the wrong tree. I'm giving it to the gas and the electric company and the landlord."

A little later, as she walked to the bus stop, Destini thought about her father. He had two personalities. Sober, he was lazy and sad and very bitter. When he drank, he was jovial and generous. Sober or drunk, you could never depend on him. By the time Destini was seven years old, he didn't live at the house anymore. She saw him about six times a year. He never seemed interested in being a husband or a father.

As soon as Destini got off the bus at school, she looked for Tyron. He was with Marko and Jasmine and some others, and they were all laughing. Destini drew close to the noisy little group. Tyron turned at once and called out, "Hey Destini, like your sweater—it's hot!"

"Thanks," Destini replied, her heart rushing. "*He likes me!*" she thought. That's what boys do when they like a girl. They give compliments. That always happened to other girls but had not happened to Destini. And now it was her turn.

Marko and Tyron went off to PE class, and Destini found herself alone with Jasmine. Jasmine intimidated her. She was so beautiful and she didn't seem real nice.

"Looks like Tyron likes you, girl," she commented.

"He's really nice," Destini responded.

27

"Well, he's got his strong points. He's really loyal to Marko. Marko couldn't have a better friend than Tyron," Jasmine offered.

"You like Marko a lot, huh Jasmine?" Destini asked.

"You know what, girl?" Jasmine asserted. "Marko can't do enough for me. He takes me to great places and buys me things. He's one awesome dude. His father, he's the man in town. He helps Marko out a lot. Now Tyron, he comes from a poor family. They got four kids and they're struggling. They live in the apartments over on Grant Street. Not such nice digs, you know?"

Destini thought it must be hard for Tyron to come from a family with financial problems. Destini's mother worked hard and earned pretty good money, so they had enough to get by.

At the end of the school day, as Destini was going to the bus stop, she saw Tyron coming toward her. "Where you off to, babe?" he asked.

"Going to take the bus home," Destini answered.

"No need to do that today," Tyron offered. "My brother has the car. Come on."

Destini walked with Tyron to an ancient Chevrolet station wagon with crunched fenders. "My brother Bennie," Tyron introduced the young man at the wheel.

"Hi Bennie," Destini greeted him.

Tyron opened the back door and got in with Destini. "You can sit with me, babe," he urged.

When the car was in motion Tyron asked, "You gotta be home right away, babe?"

"Well, Mom doesn't get in until seven, but I usually make dinner and stuff, so I should be home by six. She works really hard and she appreciates the help," Destini responded.

"That's sweet," Tyron commented. "It's going on four, so we got plenty time. Would you like to stop for something to eat? They got these great little egg rolls at a place down the street. Real cheap too."

"Sounds like fun," Destini agreed.

They crossed Grant Avenue and pulled alongside a frame building with a sign outside that read "Fish House." It was shabby looking. Geraniums used to grow in pots around the building, but somebody forgot to water them and now they were all dead.

The place wasn't bad inside but there were few customers. The three of them ordered, and the waitress brought egg rolls and sodas. Destini remembered Jasmine telling her how poor Tyron's family was, so she insisted, "I'm paying for mine."

"Okay, babe," Tyron agreed. Bennie ate twelve egg rolls, tossing them in his mouth like gum drops. He was very overweight. He was twenty years old but he looked much older.

"Like I said, Destini," Tyron started saying, "you sure do look good in that sweater. You need to wear that a lot. It really is your color. Wild cherry red."

Destini had heard boys saying things like that to girls like Sereeta and Carissa, but none ever talked to her like that. She felt amazing. "Thanks," Destini responded.

"So this is how it is" Destini thought. Having a little snack with your boyfriend, him smiling at you and giving you compliments. Feeling desirable to a boy. Feeling special.

Destini recalled reading a fairy tale when she was little. The story was about a little girl who was wandering down the street on Christmas Eve. She had nothing to eat and nowhere to go. The little girl looked in the window where there were joy and warmth but she couldn't get in. The little girl was on the outside looking in, and there was no way she could join the festivities.

That's how Destini had felt. Always outside the window where they were having fun, her heart frozen. Now, she was no longer the outsider, looking in at the pretty lights and the warmth and the dancing.

Tyron reached across the table and covered Destini's hand with his. "Look at this little hand," he urged his brother. "Isn't she a sweet little thing?"

Bennie smiled and ate some more egg rolls.

"I like you, Destini," Tyron told her. "I really like you. What do you say about that? Is it okay for me to like you? You better think long and hard about that. You think you could like me back? I wouldn't want to get close to you and then find out you didn't like me back."

"I like you too, Tyron," Destini admitted. "I've been thinking of you all the time since we talked yesterday and you gave me kind of a special look. I found your pictures in the Tubman yearbook, all those great pictures of you playing football. Boy, I never thought a football player would like me!"

"Well, a football player likes you a lot, girl," Tyron declared. He picked up her hand and kissed it. "We used to live next door to Polish people. That was their custom. The men kissed the lady's hand." Destini felt as though she had wandered into a magical kingdom.

When Bennie and Tryon dropped her off at her house, she ran inside and hurried to make dinner. They had stayed at the little restaurant longer than planned. Mom would be home in about forty-five minutes.

Destini cooked the spaghetti and cut up tomatoes and cucumbers for the salad. She found a pudding mix in the cupboard to make dessert. When her mother came in the door, everything was ready.

"Mom," Destini said, "before we eat, come and sit with me on the sofa for a minute. There's something I want to tell you. I've got news!"

Mom walked over to the sofa and sank into it, tiredly. "I may never get out of this sofa," Mom sighed, kicking off her shoes. "I am beat! So what's the news, baby?"

"Mom, I got a boyfriend. I really have a boyfriend. Can you believe it? This really nice guy said he likes me a lot and he asked me if I could like him back and I said yes, yes, yes! I'm so excited, Mom!" Destini bubbled.

Mom did not look as happy as Destini. "Who is he?" her mother demanded. "I hope he's not some thirty-year-old bum you met on the Internet."

"Oh Mom!" Destini protested. "He's a junior at Tubman, like me. His name is Tyron Becker and he's really, really nice. Oh Mom, please be happy for me, 'cause I'm walkin' on air!"

"Well, baby, just don't get carried away," Mom insisted slowly. "Just take it slow. Some boys try to take advantage of a girl, and don't you let him do that. I'm glad you're happy, child. But just be careful. Keep your eyes wide open. Just remember this. I was nineteen when I fell in love with your father, and twenty when we got married, and even at that age, I did not have sense enough to see who he truly was. I had twinkling stars in my eyes, just like you got, girl. You are sixteen years old, Destini. You are just a baby. You are *my* baby and I'm tellin' you to be careful, precious girl. You are my whole life. Y'hear what I'm saying?"

# CHAPTER THREE

When Destini went to school the next day, she ran into Alonee. "Alonee," Destini cried, "I've got a boyfriend. Tyron said he likes me. We even went out for a little date and we had egg rolls and it was so cool."

"Well," Alonee replied, "I'm happy for you if that's what you want."

Destini stared at Alonee for a moment. "You don't like Tyron, do you?" she asked.

"Oh, it's not that," Alonee protested. "He's just kind of a goof-off. I don't dislike him or anything. Maybe him hanging around Marko all the time makes him seem worse than he is. He might be okay, Destini. I don't want to rain on your parade. You might know stuff about him I don't even know."

"Oh Alonee, he's so nice," Destini said. "I mean he treats me so good. He even kissed my hand!" Destini's voice was fervent.

Alonee changed the subject. "Hey Destini, I wanted to talk to you about something. You probably heard about this group from Pastor Bromley's church. We're helping out some little foster kids."

"I heard some kids talking about taking kids out for a fun day or something," Destini acknowledged, "but I didn't pay any attention to it, Alonee."

"Well," Alonee started explaining, "we're taking six kids—three boys and three girls, about ten or eleven years old— for an overnight camping trip to the mountains. There're going to be two sets of parents to drive the vans and oversee it. We need six Tubman juniors to sort of be buddies for the kids. We've already got three boys and I'm taking a little girl, and Sami is taking another one, but we need one more girl. I was thinking. Would you like to join us, Destini?"

Destini shrugged. "What would I have to do? I'm not too good around younger kids."

"Oh, it'll be easy," Alonee declared. "Just be a friend to the girl. Sit around the campfire and talk to her, let her talk to you. Some of these kids have nobody they can really talk to. They're from foster homes and they've had really bad experiences . . . child abuse, abandonment. They need somebody just to be nice to them. It would be an overnight thing. We're leaving Friday afternoon, spending Friday night there, and coming home Saturday afternoon."

"I'd have to ask my mom," Destini said.

"Oh sure. You ask her," Alonee agreed. "We'd sure appreciate it if you could help out, Destini. I think you'd have fun too."

Destini was not eager to go on the camping trip. She thought Tyron might have plans for the weekend and she wanted to be available. Destini didn't care much for the wilderness anyway. She hated bugs, and camping out sounded dirty and dangerous. Maybe even wild animals would attack them. Destini did not want to be eaten by a mountain lion.

At home, when Destini told her mother about the camping trip, she hoped Mom would say it was a terrible idea and she couldn't go. Destini was really counting on Mom giving her a good out. But Mom gave her no excuse. "Destini, I am so proud of you that you would think about doing something like that. Most of those poor little kids have had a lot of hard knocks, and they've been through all kinds of misery. You always seemed so self-centered, girl. This just rocks me back on my heels. Baby, I am learning so much good stuff about you."

"Well, yeah, I'd like to help," Destini mumbled. "But do you think it's like dangerous to go camping in the mountains?" Destini was hoping to scare her mother into forbidding her from going. "Like, maybe there's mountain lions or snakes . . ."

Mom laughed. "Dangerous!? Baby, it's more dangerous to go down to the corner deli for a gallon of milk with the gangbangers and the drug dealers on these mean streets. I bet parents are going along on the trip and they'll make sure you got a safe place to camp without no mountain lions sniffing around."

"Well, yeah," Destini admitted. "You think I could handle some eleven-year-old kid, Mom?"

"Baby, you were eleven just a few years ago and I think you'll do just fine with that little girl," Mom assured her. "She just needs a shoulder to cry on, and you got that, Destini. If you got the heart for it, go do it!"

Destini went to her room and picked up her cell phone. "Hi Alonee, do you still need someone for that camping trip, or did you find another person already?" Destini asked.

"No, we didn't find anybody. Oh Destini, can you go? Is it okay with your mom?" Alonee asked hopefully.

"Yeah, I guess I'm in," Destini replied reluctantly. Her mother seemed so enthusiastic about the trip that Destini felt trapped. Destini knew she hadn't given her mother a lot of reasons to be proud of her and maybe she owed her this. Maybe going on the trip would make up in a small way for all the Ds and Fs on her report cards, all the griping and complaining that Destini did.

At lunchtime the next day, Tyron asked Destini to join him, Marko, and Jasmine. They all bought hotdogs in the school cafeteria. Because Mom had been so impressed with Destini going on the camping trip with the troubled kids, Destini thought Tyron might be jazzed about it too. Tyron would see what a caring person Destini was, although in Destini's heart she didn't really think she was such a nice person. She had been dragged into it. But Tyron wouldn't know that.

"I'm going on a camping trip on the weekend with a bunch of foster kids," Destini announced. "It's an outing for them and some of us juniors are going along to help. These are kids from bad homes that the child protective guys had to rescue. We're going to camp with them and roast

41

marshmallows and do all those dumb things younger kids like."

"Is that like being a camp counselor?" Marko asked. "I got a chance to do something like that this summer. How much do they pay you?"

"Oh, they don't pay anything," Destini answered. "It's a volunteer thing. Pastor Bromley came up with the idea. Six of us are doing it for nothing, you know, for the kids."

Jasmine threw back her head and laughed. "Girl, are you telling me you're going camping in the dirty, dusty old woods with six little juvenile delinquents and spending the night with them and all that for nothing? Are you wigged out or what, girl?"

Tyron added, "My father says volunteer work is sucker work. Don't do anything they're not paying you for. Only fools do volunteer work, big dopey fools. That's what my old man said." Marko started laughing too.

"They suckered you into it, didn't they?" Tyron asked. "One of those little phonies, the goody-two-shoes who act like they're out to save the world just so everybody thinks they're better than the rest of us. One of them suckered you into this, huh Destini? Who was it?"

"Well, Alonee Lennox told me about it," Destini admitted. "She said they needed one more junior for a kid." Destini began to regret agreeing to go at all.

"Alonee Lennox," Marko roared. "She is the biggest phony of them all. She's so sweet and sugar-faced, she makes me want to puke. In class she's all the time sucking up to the teachers. She's a freakin' little teacher's pet and she'd stab a kid in the back just to get in good with The Man. Poor Destini, you're a sucker."

Destini felt horrible. "I just thought I'd do it for the kid, you know, for the foster home kid." She was trying to rescue her reputation. She didn't want her precious new friends to think she was hopelessly stupid.

43

"The kid? You mean the little punk they'll stick you with?" Tyron laughed. "The kid is probably a thief and a liar. Maybe she set fire to her house and her parents dumped her on the county. She's probably a regular criminal. You be careful spending time with some little freak who's probably been in juvie enough times to learn all the dirty tricks."

Destini wished she could get out of the camping trip, but there was no way. She wouldn't have minded disappointing Alonee, but it would get back to Mom. She was friends with Alonee's mom. Destini could not stand the look of disappointment on her mom's face if she learned Destini had given her word to go on the trip and then backed out.

"Well, I won't ever do anything like this again," Destini declared. "But now I guess I'm stuck."

"Why don't you pretend you're sick?" Jasmine suggested. "Whenever I'm pushed into something I don't want to do, I play sick. Like, my grandmother is in a nursing home and Mom goes there every week. It's a horrible, ugly depressing place. I can't stand the smell. Mom thinks I should go with her. She goes, 'Oh, Grandma will be so sad if you don't come. She loves you so much,' and I go, 'Mom, my stomach hurts, you know, cramps again. Give my love to Grandma.' And Mom buys it."

"I'm always trying to get out of school by saying I'm sick, but Mom never buys it," Destini countered. "I'll just have to suffer through the camping trip this time. But it's the last time Alonee gets me into something like this."

On Friday afternoon, the parents of a classmate, Jaris Spain, picked up Destini at her home. "You got your overnight bag packed and everything you'll need, honey?" Mrs. Spain asked.

"Yeah, Alonee gave me a list of stuff I'd need. I've never done anything like this before. I think I bit off more than I can chew," Destini replied glumly.

"You'll have fun," Mrs. Spain told her. "And you're doing such a good thing too. The funny part of doing stuff like this for other people is that in the end we get more out than we give. We feel really big to be giving our time to someone who needs help, and then we look back on it and are amazed how fun it was."

Destini doubted that. She thought what Mrs. Spain had to say was a lot of bunk. She was missing out on maybe Tyron calling her for a movie or something. Just at an important time, when their friendship was growing, she was getting out of town for the weekend. How stupid was that? Maybe Tyron would be bored and he'd ask some other girl out and forget all about Destini. On top of that, Destini thought she'd probably stumble into a bed of poison ivy and be in misery for a month. And she really dreaded spending Friday afternoon and night and then Saturday with some pesky kid she didn't even know.

The other kids and chaperones were all gathered at the church when the Spains drove up. Alonee's parents were loading kids into their van. Alonee came toward Destini with a skinny kid, about eleven. The little girl had braids and big eyes, and she reminded Destini of those strange little creatures — lemurs — who live in Madagascar.

"This is Destini Fletcher," Alonee told the little girl. "Destini, this is Amber."

The girl looked down at the tops of her sneakers. Her feet seemed too small for them. Her skinny legs looked like mop sticks stuck into boat-sized shoes. The girl mumbled, "Hello."

"Hi," Destini said back.

Destini, Alonee, and Sami got into the Lennox van with the three younger girls. The Spain van was taking Jaris Spain, Kevin Walker, and Derrick Shaw and three little boys. Amber sat next to Destini in the van. Alonee was already chattering away with her young charge, and Sami and her kid were exchanging corny knock-knock jokes.

"What am I going to say to this kid?" Destini wondered. "How do I get started with this spooky little twit who won't even look at me?"

"Uh, what grade are you in at school?" Destini finally asked in desperation.

"Sixth. I'm in sixth grade," Amber replied. Her lower lip jutted out in an aggressive way. Destini recalled what Tyron had said. Amber probably was a juvenile delinquent.

"Do you like school, Amber?" Destini inquired.

"No, I hate school," Amber snarled. "I hate it. I hate it a lot."

Destini was intimidated by the venom in the girl's voice. She was such a small girl, but the rage seemed to gush from a much larger person.

Destini knew that now was the time to point out how important school was and how going to school could even be a lot of fun if you have the right attitude. Destini knew she ought to mention the nice friends you can make at school and say all the stuff parents and other adults tell kids who hate school. The trouble was that Destini herself didn't believe any of it. But she was supposed to be a role model here.

Destini shrugged and admitted, "I hate school too. I go to high school. Tubman High School. I used to be in sixth grade like you. I hated it too, but not as much as I hate high school. It just keeps getting worse the higher you go. The only fun I ever had in school was in first grade."

Amber turned to Destini, finally looking at her. "Really?" she said, her large eyes growing even larger. And that was when Destini noticed the burn scar on her forehead. It was a bad scar. It really stood out on her very dark skin.

"You looking at my scar, aren't you?" Amber remarked bitterly. "Everybody does. Makes me even uglier than I am anyways."

"You're not ugly," Destini stammered, though the truth was that Amber was not very pretty and the scar didn't help.

"Yeah, I am," the frail child insisted. "The doctor, he said he can try to fix the scar later on so it looks better. My mom's boyfriend done it. He got mad at me and he come at me with a red hot poker from the fire and he hit me with it." Amber was speaking at a rapid pace, as if trying to get the explanation over as quickly as possible. She didn't want to linger on the incident in her mind.

Destini was horror stricken. What kind of monster would do such a thing to anybody, much less a child? Still, the girl didn't seem surprised that it happened. She acted as if things like this happened frequently in her life.

"What happened to the man who hurt you?" Destini inquired.

"He got busted," Amber replied.

"That's good," Destini said.

Then Amber got back to what she was really interested in. "Do you *really* hate school, or was you just saying that?" she asked.

"Yeah, I really do hate school," Destini admitted, " 'cause it's boring. I have to sit there and listen to a lot of teachers talking about stuff I don't care about. It goes on and on, and I'm thinking about other stuff, and pretty soon they give tests and then I flunk and my mom is mad."

"I feel like that too," Amber commented. Her big eyes got a spark in them that had not been there before. The corner of her mouth twitched into a sort of smile. "But I figured maybe high school was better than sixth grade."

"No, it's worse," Destini warned. "They talk longer and they don't do any fun projects. Like one time in sixth grade we had this crazy teacher who told us to make relief maps of the universe using food. I made the planets out of plums and tomatoes and I tried to run this wire through them, but they all started falling off when I got to do my presentation."

Amber started laughing in spite of her effort to remain glum and serious. Last night, she had made up her mind that she would not like the teenager assigned to her and she would hate the trip.

Destini started giggling at the memory of her planet fiasco. "One of the plums was kinda rotten and my teacher stepped on it and almost fell down," Destini chuckled. "It was such a big mess, we never had another sixth grade project." Sami was sitting behind Destini and Amber with her young charge. She leaned over and tapped Destini on the shoulder. "You girls havin' way too much fun," she remarked, laughing.

The vans wound their way around mountain curves, coming finally to a clearing containing several log cabins. Pastor Bromley shared the location with other organizations who brought children up for weekends. They used two roomy cabins, and each had bathrooms and plenty of room for sleeping bags. Jaris's and Alonee's mothers would supervise the girl's cabin, and Jaris's and Alonee's fathers would take care of the boys.

When all the unpacking was done, everybody gathered around the fire rings outside for a cookout. There were hamburgers and hotdogs, then toasted marshmallows. Watching Amber, Destini could tell she'd never had a toasted marshmallow.

The sun was going down over the mountain ridges, and it was getting chilly. Destini overheard the men and the boys, on the other side of the fire ring, laughing and joking and telling ghost stories. She wished Tyron was among them. She liked the way Jaris, Kevin, and Derrick interacted with the younger kids. Kevin said to his boy, "When the moon comes up, then we get to hear the coyotes howl, Shawne."

"For sure?" Shawne asked, wide-eyed.

Maybe, Destini thought, if this thing didn't turn out too bad, she could talk

Tyron into getting involved. Tyron was influenced by Marko and Jasmine's attitude. Destini thought Tyron had a softer, kinder side than he showed, and she hoped she might bring that out. At first, Destini dreaded this camping trip, but now she was sort of getting into it. She even enjoyed it a little bit. In many ways, Amber was like Destini had been at that age, and that made Destini feel close to her.

As they sat by the fire, Amber asked, "Are you smart in anything in school, Destini?"

"No," Destini allowed. Then she thought about the question. "Maybe art."

"I'm bad in most everything," Amber replied. "But I *love* math."

"Math!" Destini almost choked on her marshmallow. "You *like* math. Math is horrible. It's impossible to understand."

"No it's not," Amber insisted. "It's easy. It's like a game. I jump ahead in the book and do the harder problems. I'm doing some algebra."

"Oh wow," Destini cried, "I never met a girl who likes math. You are amazing. People who're good at math are so lucky. That's because a lot of us struggle with it, and the world needs teachers who can get it through our thick heads."

Amber grinned. She wasn't used to praise of any kind.

"You know what?" Destini went on to say. "Maybe when I'm having trouble understanding something in math, you could help me. You know, tutor me."

"You'd let *me* tutor *you*? But I'm only eleven and you're sixteen," Amber said.

"That doesn't matter," Destini countered. "If you're good in math, I'd really appreciate it if you gave me some help."

"You think?" Amber probed in an almost reverential voice. "Or you just jiving?"

"For sure," Destini asserted.

When they were all in their sleeping bags, beyond the cabin windows a large moon began to rise from behind the mountain. As it sailed into the open sky, the soft yips and then drawn-out howls of the coyotes filled the night.

"Shawne!" Kevin whispered, in the boys' cabin. "Listen. There they are. The coyotes."

"Whoa!" Shawne said back in a hushed voice.

In the other cabin, Destini also heard the howls and decided she wasn't too crazy about coyotes. Amber was curled up in her sleeping bag beside Destini, and she opened her big eyes and whispered, "Whatever is makin' that awful noise can't get in here with us, can it?"

"No Amber," Destini assured her, reaching over and giving the girl's shoulder a squeeze.

# CHAPTER FOUR

In the morning, they all went hiking. Destini and Amber caught up to Derrick Shaw and his boy, Josh. All four of them took off their shoes and socks and went wading in a cold mountain stream along the trail.

"Oooooo, that feels good, huh Josh?" Derrick suggested. "Hey Josh, look at the little pollywogs slithering around down there."

Josh and Amber both scampered over to where Derrick was pointing.

"They look like funny fish," Josh commented. "Can we catch some of them?"

"No," Derrick said. "When they grow up they'll be frogs. Now they're baby frogs. You don't want them not to grow up and be like Kermit on TV." Derrick laughed at his own joke. "Besides, we got a teacher at Tubman High who'd horsewhip us if we captured baby frogs."

"Could he do that?" Josh asked.

"I dunno," Derrick mused. "I don't want to find out."

They all scrambled from the water then and sat in a grassy spot beneath an old tree. Destini didn't know Derrick, but she had seen kids making fun of him because he was slow. Destini was surprised at how well he was getting along with Josh. He didn't seem stupid after all.

Derrick was looking at Destini at the same moment she was looking at him. "I'm real surprised to see you here," he remarked.

"I'm surprised to see you too," Destini told him. "But how come you're surprised to see me?"

Derrick shrugged. "You seem mad at school all the time, Destini," he explained.

"You seem stuck up too. And when Marko Lane makes fun of people, like Mr. Pippin or me, you laugh. It made me think you were one of those mean girls. You don't expect to see a mean girl helping out with these kids."

"Destini is not mean," Amber said. "She's all right."

"Well," Derrick said, "you don't seem mean now." He looked more intently at Destini and asked her, "How come you were surprised to see me here?"

Destini felt bad saying it, but she did anyway. "I guess because a lot of kids say you're dumb and stuff. I thought you were dull witted or something, but you're not. I didn't think such a dumb guy could be with the kids, but you're doing fine. I just didn't expect you to be just a regular guy . . ."

"I'm no genius or anything, but I get by," Derrick responded. "I'm going to graduate from Tubman with a C, I think. I'm not as dumb as I look sometimes, or as Marko Lane and his buddies make me out to be. I don't know why they do that. I've never done anything to them . . . "

Destini looked down into the meadow grass for a moment. What Derrick said made her sad. She didn't much like Marko either, but she liked Tyron and Tyron and Marko were close friends. Because Tyron thought so much of Marko, Destini couldn't be disloyal to Marko either. "I think Marko is just joking around," she offered. "I don't think he means to hurt people . . . "

On Saturday afternoon, as the vans pulled into the church parking lot, everybody was saying they were sorry the day was ending. Destini felt that way too, but she wasn't ready yet to admit that. She never would say so when she got home and got a call from Tyron.

"You're finally home from the nightmare, eh babe?" Tyron asked.

"Yeah," Destini answered. "All done."

"Did the little monster you were stuck with try to push you over a cliff or anything?" Tyron joked.

"No, that part was okay. She was a good kid," Destini said.

"Let's see," Tyron went on. "It's five o'clock. Is it too late for us to go to the movies?"

Destini was tired. She wasn't used to all that hiking. She had fun yesterday and today, but she was worn out. She hadn't even had time to shower. Her hair was a mess. "Maybe we could make it tomorrow," Destini responded.

"Hey babe, you got time for those little squid, but you're blowing me off. I'm lonely for you, Destini. I'm dying to see you. You hear what I'm saying?" Tyron urged.

"Okay, yeah, just give me forty-five minutes," Destini agreed. "I'd love to see a movie with you, Tyron, after I get the dust out of my hair."

"That's more like it, babe," he said. "See you at six. Bennie'll drive us."

Destini raced into the bathroom and showered. She struggled to make her wet hair manageable. She thought it looked like a big black tumbleweed.

"What are you tearing around for, girl?" Mom asked. "You just got home."

"Oh Mom, my boyfriend, Tyron, he called and he's taking me to the movies," Destini explained.

"*What*?" Mom gasped. "You been campin' for two days and now you're goin' to the movies? Don't he know what a day you had?" Mom sounded annoyed.

"He says he's lonely for me, Mom," Destini responded. "I don't want to disappoint him. He's really nice."

"Girl, I don't like this," Mom grumbled. "This boy sounds like he's real domineering. He don't care how much he puts you out, as long as he gets what he wants. A considerate boy wouldn't have even asked you out after you put in a day and a half camping."

"It's okay, Mom," Destini assured her. "I really want to go to the movies with Tyron."

A little after six, Bennie drove up in front of the house. Bennie hit the horn. A frown came over Destini's mother's face. "I see," Mom snapped. "He's one of those. One of them boys who don't have the courtesy to come inside and say hello. That makes me sick. That makes me really sick. He honks and the girl is supposed to come running like a dog or something."

"Mommm," Destini groaned. "It's just that we're running late and he wants to get to the theater." Destini ran past her mother, down the walk to the car. Sitting inside, Tyron held the back door open and Destini hopped in.

Destini's legs ached from all the hiking. She had dreamed of a nice long soak in the bathtub. She planned to go to bed early and have a good night's sleep. She didn't feel like a movie and she was only going for Tyron.

"We're gonna see *Saw Town*, baby," Tyron announced. Bennie laughed from the driver's seat and said, "Yeah, they say it makes those chainsaw movies seem tame."

Destini hated horror movies. She liked comedies and musicals. One time she went to a horror movie with two girlfriends, and she couldn't sleep for a week. She kept sitting up in the dark and imagining hideous strangers with claws for hands entering her bedroom.

"Yeah?" she said now.

"Yeah," Tyron went on. "See, in this movie, these guys trap tourists staying at this creepy hotel, and they get them down to the basement and—zzzzzz!—the saws go to work. I bet after spending a coupla days with those stupid delinquents you wouldn't mind feeding them to the saws."

"They weren't bad, the kids I mean," Destini replied. "But I'm glad the day is over." Destini did not mean to say that but she knew it was what Tyron wanted to hear, so she said it. What troubled her a little was that she was spending so much effort saying things she didn't believe just to please Tyron. But she cared for him and he cared for her, and it was worth it.

"So who else from Tubman was at that stupid camp thing?" Tyron asked.

"Alonee and Sami were the other girls. Jaris Spain and Derrick Shaw were there. And Kevin, the guy from Texas." Destini listed them.

"Derrick Shaw?" Tyron asked. "Man, he's so stupid it's a wonder they let him come along. He's almost one of those special needs guys."

"No Tyron, he did okay. He hiked and played softball and did everything the rest of us did," Destini countered.

"You almost sound like you had a good time, babe," Tyron remarked. "Like you enjoy hanging out with phonies like Jaris and Alonee."

"Oh no, I got trapped into it," Destini said quickly. Again, Destini felt funny. Never before in her life did she feel obliged to say things she didn't believe just to please someone.

"Here we are," Bennie declared, parking in front of a ratty looking movie house.

They showed old horror movies and minor films that nobody really wanted to see.

The theater smelled of rancid popcorn. It was sparsely attended, with many of the customers looking like homeless men who had come in for a place to sit down. There were a lot of seats in the middle, but Tyron led them up front. "I like the action in my lap," Tyron stated.

Bennie went to get them popcorn even though Destini didn't want any, especially the way the place smelled. Destini had eaten so much on the camping trip she felt stuffed, but soon Tyron was shoving the box of buttered popcorn at her. When she didn't join in reaching into the box, Tyron urged her. "Hey eat up, girl. We got the extra deluxe buttered popcorn just for you. It wasn't cheap."

It was the most disgusting movie Destini had ever seen. There was so much blood and gore she thought she was going to vomit. But most of the guys in the theater were laughing and yelling, including

Bennie and Tyron. As heads and body parts flew through the air, the roars of approval increased. Destini closed her eyes often and kept telling herself that this is the kind of stuff guys like and girls don't. Guys were different than girls when it came to movies. Guys thrived on violence.

"It kinda scared me," Destini admitted as they walked out of the theater after the movie. "I mean, horror movies like that make my skin crawl."

"You'd of rather gone to a chick flick where everybody gets out their hankies and weeps, huh, babe?" Tyron asked, laughing.

"I guess," Destini said. She was so tired she hoped she wouldn't fall asleep in the car on the way home. When they pulled up to Destini's house, Tyron and Destini got out of the car and walked to the door. Tyron reached out and took her hand. "Hey beautiful," he asked softly, "do I get a goodnight kiss?"

Destini turned numb. *Beautiful*? He called her "beautiful." Her weariness vanished and she turned to him smiling. Tyron bent down and kissed Destini gently on the lips, and she reached up and caressed his cheek. She had never felt to special in all her life. She felt like Cinderella when the prince discovered her dainty foot was a fit for the golden slipper.

"Goodnight Tyron," Destini said at the door.

"Goodnight beautiful," he whispered in her ear.

Destini stood there watching them drive away. She kept asking herself, "Did he really call me beautiful? Did he really, *really* call me beautiful. Me of the frizzy hair, the plain face?" Destini was not Sereeta or Alonee or Carissa. Everyone knew they were beautiful. She was Destini Fletcher, always the outsider, never the chosen one. But now she had been chosen.

Destini went inside. She heard her mother turn off her bedside light. She had been up waiting for Destini's safe return. Now Mom could go to sleep.

CHAPTER FOUR

In her room, Destini sat in front of the bedroom mirror for a few moments. She looked at the image of herself. How could he have called her beautiful? But he did. He did. And she loved him for that. She loved him with all her heart.

At school on Monday, the first person Destini saw was Derrick Shaw. He looked fantastic. "Did you get the word yesterday?" he asked.

"What word?" Destini asked back.

"There's gonna be a surprise quiz in English. I didn't read half the stories. I'm doomed!" Derrick groaned.

"Oh Derrick, that can't be!" Destini responded. "Mr. Pippin always tells us when he's having a test." Just then Destini caught sight of Marko and Tyron laughing like crazy a few yards away. She knew they had sent Derrick the message. "Don't worry, Derrick. It's just a joke. There isn't going to be any test," she assured him.

Derrick saw where Destinit was looking, turned, and saw the two boys. "They put the word out, didn't they? I worried all night about it." An angry look came to Derrick's face. "Why would they do something like that?" He shook his head, stuffed his hands in his pockets and walked away.

Destini walked over to Marko and Tyron.

"Did he wet his pants?" Marko asked. "He looked freaked enough to wet his pants!"

"Marko, that was mean," Destini declared.

"It was funny," Tyron cried. "We had him going for a minute, didn't we? But then you came along and spoiled it, Destini. He's such a big joke. It's fun to yank his chain."

Destini tried to smile, but her face wouldn't cooperate. "Please Tyron, I mean, I know you wouldn't do something like that, but Marko puts you up to it," she told him.

"I'm a bad influence on you Tyron," Marko whimpered in a mock hurt voice.

"I'm a baaad boy. You better not hang with me, Tyron. You better go hang with the goody-goodies like Jaris. I make you do bad things."

Tyron laughed and turned to Destini. "Lunch today, beautiful? The food's not good, but the company is great."

Destini was trying to follow Ms. McDowell's advice to study more and bring up her grades. That was important to Mom too. That morning, at breakfast, Mom had said, "Destini, unless you bring up your grades, you are going to get grounded. I mean it, girl. No more Ds are gonna pass muster around here. I wanna see a few Bs, nothin' worse than a C. If you got the time to hang with that creepy boy, then you got the time to study, you hear what I'm saying to you?"

"Mom," Destini had protested, "he's not a creepy boy. He likes me. He thinks I'm pretty. Do you know what that means to me? Most of the boys at Tubman look at me like I'm part of the sidewalk, but he looks into my eyes and he cares about me."

Destini brought her binder to English and was prepared to take notes.

"Today we are dealing with points of view," Mr. Pippin lectured. "Some stories use an objective point of view. They do not go into the minds of the characters. 'The Wish Book' by George Milburn is such a story."

Marko raised his hand. "What's the wish book, Mr. Pippin? I read the story but I couldn't figure out what the wish book was. Could you explain that?" he asked.

Mr. Pippin looked at Marko. He knew the boy too well to think he was asking a sincere question. He regarded Marko as a snake always ready to strike. "Why it's a mail order catalogue. That's quite obvious."

"But it says the wish book sold sizzle pants, and I've never seen sizzle pants in a mail order catalogue," Marko went on. He was starting to laugh. On cue, Tyron and a couple others were laughing too. "What *are* sizzle pants?"

"Yeah," Tyron added. "We have to know what these sizzle pants are in order to understand the story. Have you ever worn sizzle pants, Mr. Pippin?" Tyron's voice was gurgling with laughter.

Mr. Pippin flushed. "They are simply trousers that people wore at the time. Now, for the point of view—"

"Do they sizzle? Like bacon in a frying pan?" Marko asked. " 'Cause that'd be hard if your pants sizzled."

Mr. Pippin's face twisted in rage. "Marko Lane, Tyron Becker, and Eddie North, get up and leave my classroom at once. You will be scheduled for detention all of this week and the next," he declared.

"Aw Mr. Pippin, we were just trying to lighten things up," Marko whined.

"Get out of my classroom now and report to the vice principal in charge of discipline," Mr. Pippin asserted.

Marko began to look concerned. "I can't do detention. I got track and football practice," he said seriously.

"I don't care," Mr. Pippin almost screamed. "Out! Out!"

Destini felt terrible. She glanced back at Tyron. He'd miss football practice too. It could threaten his position on the team. After the three boys left, the class continued. It was tense but orderly.

After class, Destini saw Marko and his friends near the vice principal's office. "This is gonna ruin me on the track team. Coach Curry will use it as an excuse to throw me off the relay team," Marko stormed.

"That old fool Pippin," Tyron raged. "Where does he come off doing something like this? I wish he'd drop dead. He's old enough."

Destini felt cold all over. "Oh Tyron, don't say that," she warned. "Please don't say things like that."

"I'll say anything I want," Tyron snapped.

# CHAPTER FIVE

"**P**ippin's not fit to teach," Marko declared. "Everybody knows that. He's senile. He doesn't know what he's talking about, and he blames us that the class is a mess all the time. I'm gonna make a petition and take it to the principal. I'm gonna tell him how this creep isn't fit to teach and he's gotta be kicked out and sent to a nursing home where he belongs."

"Yeah," Tyron said excitedly. "We'll all sign the petition."

Destini saw Mr. Pippin clutching his worn briefcase talking to Ms. McDowell near the library. He looked distraught. It was clear that Ms. McDowell was trying to reassure him. He appeared to be shaking.

It was the first time he had taken serious action against his tormentors, and he feared the consequences.

Marko walked into a group of students trying to get signatures for his petition. Jaris Spain saw what he was doing and said, "Are you crazy, Marko? Do you think anybody who wasn't stupid would sign that petition? Yeah, Mr. Pippin isn't the greatest teacher in the world, but he's okay. You and your friends are the problem in that class. I'd rather sign a petition to get rid of you guys."

"Give it up, Lane," Kevin Walker added. "Everybody knows you've been acting like a freakin' fool in that class. Grow up, man."

"Come on, you guys," Jasmine argued. "Why are you siding with a teacher instead of the students? Mr. Pippin needs to go. He's older than dirt!"

Alonee glared at Jasmine. "Jaz, you're a good student. You make good grades. Don't throw in with those goof-offs," she urged.

Jasmine ignored Alonee. She handed the petition to Destini and said, "We got five signatures already. You can be number six, girl."

Destini stared at the petition. She didn't want to sign it. What if Mr. Pippin found out who signed the petition against him? Maybe he would flunk all the students who signed. Destini was not sure if he could do that or not. She was afraid to take the chance. "Tyron, look," she said, dodging the issue, "hardly anybody is signing. I don't think it's going to work."

Tyron's face showed a mixture of surprise and anger. "Babe, you are telling me you won't sign it? You won't back me up? That detention is gonna mess up my life, babe. He's gonna hurt me big time, that old devil," Tyron demanded.

"It's just that I've never signed a petition against a teacher, Tyron," Destini explained. "I'm scared."

Tyron grabbed Destini's wrist. He grabbed it so hard that an ache went up to

Destini's shoulder. "You sign this, Destini, or else you're saying I don't matter that much to you. If you really loved me you would sign it right off."

"Ow, you're hurting me!" Destini cried.

Derrick was standing nearby. He turned and came closer. "Let go of her, dude," he growled. "She said you're hurting her."

"I don't need a moron like you to tell me how to act with my girl," Tyron snapped. He turned to Destini, "Was I hurting you, babe?" He was smiling at her but it wasn't his usual nice smile.

"No," Destini mumbled. She knew Tyron did not mean to grasp her wrist so hard. He would never do anything to hurt her. He was just so upset, and he was so strong that he didn't realize his own strength.

Tyron thrust the petition at Destini and she signed it quickly. Tyron smiled at her again. "Atta girl," he smiled. "We gotta stick together against that old fool, Pippin. He's out to get us, but we'll get him first."

Tyron took the petition and walked away, saying, "See you later, beautiful."

When Tyron was gone, Derrick walked over. "I don't like that guy, Destini," he warned her. "Be careful."

"Oh, he's nice. He just gets upset sometimes," Destini explained.

Derrick shrugged. "Suit yourself, but if you were my sister I'd be doing something."

Destini looked after Derrick. He just didn't understand Tyron. It touched Destini that Derrick was concerned about her, even though his help was not necessary. Derrick was a nice guy, much more fun than Destini had thought he was. Before they were on that camping trip together, Destini didn't realize Derrick had a good sense of humor and a lot of heart.

Destini was sorry she had signed the petition, but she didn't think she had had a choice. Tyron would have been terribly hurt if she had refused. Destini just hoped that things would turn out all right and that Mr. Pippin would not retaliate against the petitioners.

Destini went to American History I and took her usual place. Since Ms. McDowell had talked to her, she was striving very hard to take good notes and read all the assigned material. Destini thought that if she worked really hard, she might get a B in history. That would make Mom really happy.

Destini hoped it would never get to Ms. McDowell that she had signed the petition against Mr. Pippin. Destini wondered if teachers go to the faculty room at breaks and talk about the students, as students talk about their teachers. She supposed they did. "Oh, do you have that stupid kid in your class too? . . . Oh my, yes. I dread to see her come in!"

When Destini began to take notes in class, her sore right wrist reminded her of Tyron's grasp. She hadn't realized he grabbed her that hard, but he was a football player and he no doubt had no idea what he had done. Tyron was used to being rough, and for a minute he forgot he was dealing with his girlfriend, not a runningback from the opposing team.

After history, Alonee caught up to Destini. "He pressured you to sign that stupid petition, didn't he?" Alonee asked.

"No, I wanted to," Destini lied. "I mean, Mr. Pippin is too old to teach, don't you think? Teachers should be, uh . . . younger, so they understand the kids better. I mean, he came down really hard on those boys when they didn't do anything so bad."

Alonee seemed to be looking right through Destini, into her brain, and she detected the lies. "Destini, people heard you telling Tyron you were afraid to sign the petition, and then he grabbed your arm and—" Alonee started to say.

"No, he didn't. Whoever told you that is lying," Destini said passionately. "He didn't touch me. I just changed my mind because I thought harder about it. I decided that I shouldn't let being afraid stop me from doing the right thing." Destini then tried to change the subject. "That was a good lecture in history today. All the teachers should be like Ms. McDowell. She's really good."

"Destini," Alonee persisted, "you have to promise me something. If any boy ever hurts you, or if you're afraid of a guy . . . I mean if he hits you or anything . . . you'll get away fast and ask for help. Okay? I know you care a lot for Tyron, but if anything bad happens, you'll get help, right?"

"Oh, Tyron would never hurt me," Destini asserted. "I know there are guys like that out there, but Tyron is so gentle. He's a really good person, Alonee. I'm not foolish enough to have anything to do with a boy who'd hurt me. I mean, that's just crazy." Destini knew she was talking too fast and protesting too much, but she was nervous.

After school, Tyron saw Destini walking toward the bus stop. He called out, "Destini, wait a minute."

Destini turned and waited for him. When he reached her, Destini greeted him. "How's it going, Tyron?"

"I got that lousy detention," Tyron replied, "but it doesn't start for a few minutes. I just wanted to give you something. It's no big deal but I just wanted you to have it." He handed her an envelope. There was a paper inside, and on the paper was a poem. It looked like a page had been torn from a book. "I saw this today," he told her. "It reminded me of you. I wanted you to have it, babe."

"Oh Tyron," Destini sighed, giving him a hug. She put the poem in her binder to read later. She would have kissed Tyron right there, but a lot of kids were around. She didn't want to put on a show for them.

"That's you in the poem, girl," Tyron said. Then he turned and hurried toward detention. Destini felt so sorry for him.

On the bus, Destini took the poem out of her binder and read it. It was titled

"To a Fair Maiden of My Heart's Desire."
Her heart racing, Destini read the poem,

She is lovely as a rose, she is my dearest
treasure,

She is the one I chose, loved beyond all
measure,

I thank the fates that brought us
together.

The author of the poem was listed as
anonymous.

The poem came from a book that was
maybe trying to teach poetry. But the
sentiment in the poem touched Destini
deeply. She read it over and over, amazed
that this was how Tyron felt about her.
She never thought he was the sort of a boy
who would read a poem, much less apply
one so sentimental to their friendship. She
would take the poem home and put it in
her diary. She would date the entry and
tell in detail how Tyron had given it to her
and what he said. Tenderly now, Destini
put the page containing the precious poem
back in her binder.

Destini had been documenting her entire friendship with Tyron in her diary. From that first moment in English class when Tyron made eye contact with her, everything was lovingly written down. The egg rolls and even the horror movie were there. The diary was the evidence that she, Destini Fletcher, at last had a real boyfriend. Now she added the poem on the page torn from a book. This was surely the most tender evidence of their growing friendship.

Alonee called that evening. "Destini, we're taking the kids to a movie on Friday night. It's that new animated movie about seagulls. It's supposed to be awesome. Want to come? We'll be home before eleven," she said.

Destini thought for a moment. "Will Amber be there?" she asked. Destini had bonded with Amber. She liked the little girl. She wanted their friendship to continue.

"Yeah," Alonee responded. "Amber's one of the kids."

"Okay. I can go," Destini agreed.

"Pastor Bromley has a big van and he'll pick you up, Destini. There's room for all of us in the van. Thanks a lot. It'll mean a lot to Amber that you're coming. She asked if you'd be there. Now I can tell her you will be," Alonee told her.

Destini smiled to herself. Most everyone she knew came from a family with several kids. Destini wanted a brother or a sister—one at least—preferably a sister. She would be so jealous when she'd see little girls looking up to their big sisters or big sisters helping the younger ones. Amber was now sort of the little sister she never had. What made it extra special was that Amber was so much like Destini. She was a little rebel who refused to pretend everything was okay when it wasn't.

"Mom, I'm going to the movies Friday night with that group from the church," Destini said when her mother got home from work. "Pastor Bromley is driving us and we'll be home before eleven. I'll be able to spend time with that little girl I told you about—Amber."

"That's the child got burned by that devil of a boyfriend her mother brought home, isn't it?" Mom recalled. "I'm tellin' you, girl, there must be a hot place in hell for men who abuse women and children. At least your father never done that. I can truthfully say, he never laid a violent hand on me or you. The man couldn't hurt a fly. He's no account and lazy, but there's no meanness in him. That counts for something in my book."

"Amber is a neat kid, Mom," Destini confessed. "We really clicked. I like her a lot."

"Bless your heart, child. I'm sure having a friend like you is gonna mean the world to that poor little girl," Mom said with feeling. Destini knew Mom was really proud of her for what she was doing. Destini knew that she hadn't been the best kid around and that she gave her mom a lot of grief. It felt good now to be doing something Mom liked because Destini did love her mother very much. Mom was the one who took care of Destini all these years with no help from Dad. If not for Mom, Destini figured she'd be stuck in some foster home like Amber with people who weren't connected to her. Until she met Tyron, Destini thought nobody in the world cared if she lived or died except for Mom. Now there was Mom and Tyron.

Later that night, Destini wondered if the petition against Mr. Pippin had gotten anywhere. She hoped somebody had just dumped it in the trash before Mr. Pippin had even seen it. She thought that was probably what happened. Principals didn't care what kids thought of their teachers, and, anyway, Mr. Pippin's job was secure. He'd been there so long he had tenure.

At school the next day, Destini asked Jasmine about the petition. Jasmine said that Marko had taken it to the principal's office and left it there.

"How many kids ended up signing it?" Destini asked.

"About ten from the English class," Jasmine replied. "That means twenty were too chicken to sign even though they all know Mr. Pippin isn't fit to teach. Can you beat that? Marko was trying to do something for all of us, and most of those fools wouldn't even back him up."

"Maybe a lot of the kids felt sorry for Mr. Pippin," Destini suggested. "He is pretty old. It must be terrible to be old like that and trying to teach kids who don't like you."

"If he was any good, he'd quit," Jasmine insisted. "He must be a selfish old man to stay where he's not wanted."

When it was time for English class, Destini wondered if Mr. Pippin would even show up. He looked so upset the last time she saw him that she thought maybe he had a heart attack or a nervous breakdown. But just before class started, there was Mr. Pippin with his old briefcase taking his place behind his desk. He looked more weary than usual. Then, a few seconds later, another man came into the room and sat in the last row. It was Mr. Hawthorne, the vice principal. He sat just behind Marko and Tyron. Mr. Hawthorne was about forty, good-looking, with wire-rimmed glasses. He carried a clipboard. Destini thought he had come to observe Mr. Pippin's class and to see if he was as bad as some of the students said he was.

Destini glanced back and noticed Marko and Tyron were smirking. They smelled victory in the air. Mr. Pippin was being evaluated. He was under the gun, and he would fail miserably because he was such a bad teacher. Then they would give him some paper-pushing job downtown, and a new English teacher would be hired.

Marko looked triumphant. In a few minutes, he thought, Mr. Hawthorne would see what an incompetent and demented man old Pippin was. Marko had made it happen, and he swelled with pride.

"Here, in today's story, 'A Red Letter Day,' " Mr. Pippin began class, his voice cracking, then quickly recovering, "we have a mother and son. It should be a touching story of a lonely boy eager to spend time with his mother away from the boarding school where he lives. His mother should be equally happy to be spending some precious time with her boy, an opportunity to be with her beloved son. But is this what the story is really about?"

Jaris raised his hand. "No, it's about this woman who doesn't know how to be a mother," he said.

Alonee joined in. "The mother loves her son as well as she can, but she doesn't feel comfortable with him."

"Ah," Mr. Pippin said, his voice now full and rich, "why is that?"

Kevin Walker poked his hand in the air and spoke up. "The mother is kind of immature. She sees this other lady at the boarding school picking up her kids, and this other lady is really mothering. She's happy and jovial and easy with her kids, but the other mom in the story feels strange with her kid."

Derrick Shaw raised his hand. Everyone turned to look at Derrick. Usually when he made a comment, it wasn't very good. It was often stupid and off the mark. Now he said, "It says in the story that the mother felt guilty."

Everybody held their breath as Mr. Pippin asked gently, "Why do you think she felt guilty, Derrick?"

"Uh, well, I kinda think, you know, her husband left her and she was looking for guys, and, uh . . . I guess she felt guilty that she needed to look for guys instead of taking care of her kid."

"Yes!" Mr. Pippin enthused. "The author touches on a very modern dilemma— divorced parents. How much time must they spend with their children? And do they have a right to social lives of their own? Can they spend time dating if it means being away from the children? Or must they devote their lives to being parents even though this means they might be lonely in their middle and later years? This story was written in 1948—so many years ago—and yet it speaks to us today. It proves that good literature is time-less . . . you see?"

Destini was amazed. She never saw Mr. Pippin in such good form. She glanced back a couple times and saw Mr. Hawthorne jotting down comments on his clipboard. Mr. Hawthorne looked interested and pleased. Mr. Pippin had ceased being a beleaguered old man, hounded to bumbling confusion by his students. He was now a confident teacher leading a good class discussion.

"As Derrick rightly pointed out," Mr. Pippin went on, "this mother was torn between her child and her yearning for, as she put it, 'those emotional adventures,' the tenuous grasping after life.''

Marko looked dumbfounded by the turn of events.

Mr. Hawthorne left a few moments before class ended with a nod and a hearty, "Thank you, Mr. Pippin."

Standing outside the classroom, Marko said, "The old fake pulled it off. He was putting on an act all through class. He's never like that . . . usually."

"Yeah," Jaris pointed out. "Because you and your buddies are always playing fools and messing him up, but today, with Mr. Hawthorne watching, you didn't dare. The poor man got a chance to really teach for a change—and he did a good job."

"Stuff it in your ear, Spain," Marko snarled bitterly. Tyron stood loyally beside Marko. They were closer than brothers, Destini thought again. Loyalty was a virtue, wasn't it? But what was Tyron being loyal to?

Later that day, Destini had lunch with Tyron, just the two of them. Alonee and Sami had asked Destini to join them for lunch, but she said she had other plans.

Destini and Tyron went to a little corner of the campus under the eucalyptus trees and sat on the grass. Mom had packed a ham and cheese sandwich for Destini, with a lot of pickle relish, just the way Destini liked it. It occurred to Destini, as it had so often, that her mother never skipped the little things like knowing what Destini liked for lunch.

Destini thought about the story in English. Her mom was nothing like the mother in that story. Mom was a mother, all the time, every time.

# CHAPTER SIX

Tyron got a sandwich from the machine. Destini had tried them once. They were like dry cheese between cardboard slices.

"How long have you and Marko been friends?" Destini asked Tyron.

"Oh man, we go way back," Tyron replied. "We always had each other's backs. Marko is a great guy. His daddy is real generous too. He's an operator, I'm telling you. He's got a lot of irons in the fire. Marko shares with me. Uh, my folks aren't doing so good. Never did. Like when we were little kids, I'd never have gotten to go to Disneyland or Six Flags—those places—except Marko's father took him and me too."

"My family is sort of like that too," Destini admitted. "I haven't ever been to Six Flags, and the only time I went to Disneyland was on a school trip. And then my dad took me once to Knott's Berry Farm. My dad doesn't live with us. He won some money at the races that time and took me. I was so excited, but my father drank too much and Mom had to come get me."

"My father doesn't drink," Tyron responded. "But he's a loser, you know. A big loser. He quit high school and he can't do nothin'. He gets these nickel-and-dime jobs. Makes chump change. Mom works too, but she has crummy jobs. If it wasn't for Marko I'd miss out on a lot of stuff. He even let me have his cell phone when the new ones came out and he got one of them. And he had this cool camera, and he gave it to me when his father got him the new one with all the latest stuff. It was great to have his old camera, I'm tellin' you."

"I'm glad he helps you, Tyron," Destini commented.

"Yeah, and I pay him back by sticking with him—no matter what," Tyron said excitedly. "Marko is really popular, Destini. He's the most popular guy here at school. I'm proud to be his best friend. Some guys are jealous of him. They give him a hard time because he's so popular and, you know, good-looking."

"You're good-looking too," Destini asserted. "I think you're really handsome."

Tyron grinned. "Ahhh," he patted his stomach. "I need to work off somma this bad boy belly, like Marko, and get lean and mean like him. I got this spare tire like my old man already. I don't want to look like him. Man, he's a mess, babe. He's only forty-eight or something, and he sits there at the kitchen table with no shirt on and this big stomach. He looks like a beached whale. I got to get in shape so I don't end up like him."

"Most men, when they get older, put on weight," Destini said comfortingly. "My father hasn't much, but he's kinda in poor health. He doesn't eat good and he drinks."

"You should see Marko's father," Tyron said, his face shining with admiration. "What a classy dude. He's as trim as a kid. That's where Marko gets his looks. When Marko's dad goes by with those gold chains he wears, a lot of ladies turn their heads."

"I wonder what'll happen now in English class," Destini said, changing the subject.

"Old Pippin dodged the bullet," Tyron responded. "He put on that show for Hawthorne and I think we're stuck with the old buzzard. The one I really feel sorry for is Marko. Just because old Pippin hates him, he got him detention, and now Marko is missing some important track practice. That's so unfair. That Coach Curry on the track team, he plays favorites anyway. He's got it in for Marko. He likes that creepy Texan, Walker. So now Marko isn't practicing and Curry'll try to dump him from the team and it's all Pippin's fault. Pippin ruining a guy's life like that just because he's a spiteful old man."

Destini looked down at the grass as she finished her sandwich. She wondered if Tyron ever thought it was wrong for Marko to deliberately disrupt Mr. Pippin's class with his antics. He did everything he could to throw the teacher off his stride. He scraped his chair along, coughed when he didn't need to, asked stupid questions to ruin the discussions.

"Tyron," Destini asked cautiously, "why does Marko do stuff in class to, you know, cause trouble?"

Tyron looked right at Destini. "You mean like goofing around a little?" he replied. "Ah, he's so bored. We all are. We gotta do something to break the monotony. You know, like he did when he was pretending to swat that mosquito. You gotta admit that was funny. You were laughing, babe. Don't deny it. If stuff like that didn't happen once in a while, we'd all dry up of boredom and blow away."

"But sometimes," Destini went on, still cautiously, "it seems like Marko is being mean. Like to Derrick Shaw. That poor guy. Like when he fell down at the library and Marko made fun of him. I don't know . . ."

"Do you *like* Derrick Shaw, Destini?" Tyron asked.

"Oh no," Destini said too quickly, almost defensively, "nobody does. But I sometimes feel sorry for him 'cause everybody says he's stupid, and when Marko does stuff like that it's like piling it on, you know? At the camping trip the other day, he said like he's really hurt by some of the teasing . . . "

"Ah, you're too sensitive, Destini," Tyron said. "We gotta laugh at stupid people. When they're as stupid as Derrick, it doesn't bother them as much as it would with a normal person. Marko doesn't mean any harm. That's just his way."

Destini shrugged. "Maybe so, but I don't think we should make fun of people. Maybe they act as if they don't care, but I think they do."

"You know what, babe?" Tyron said. "I bet you got something going with Derrick.

If you didn't like him, why would you care what was going on with him? I bet you got a crush on that big, stupid moron."

"Oh Tyron, don't be silly," Destini protested. "I don't like him the least bit. You're the one I'm crazy about."

Tyron smiled. "Did you like the poem I gave you, babe?"

"I pasted it in my diary and every night I read it over and over, Tyron," Destini cooed. "It's the nicest thing anybody ever gave me. I felt so special that you think of me like that."

When the bell rang for the end of lunch, Destini and Tyron got up. Tyron reached for Destini's hand. Very gently he pulled her toward him, brushing a kiss across her forehead. "You *are*," he whispered.

"What?" Destini asked.

"Beautiful," Tyron said. "You are beautiful."

Destini giggled happily, gathered up her books and hurried to her next class.

When Destini got home from school that day, someone was already in the house. Mom's old Toyota wasn't in the driveway, but she knew somebody was in the house. Destini did not go right in. She peeked in the front window and saw her father sitting on the couch in the living room.

Destini went in. The door was unlocked. He never locked doors.

"Hi Dad," Destini greeted him. "You watching TV?"

"Well, I'm sitting here and the TV is on, so I guess that's what I'm doing," he responded. "I was kicked out of that apartment where I was roommates with Thor and Jack. I figured I'd crash here for a while. You know that money I won on the ponies the other day? I gave your mother some and said for her to throw a few bucks your way. Any of that left? I could use it."

"It's all gone," Destini replied. "Mom paid some bills and I bought a new sweater."

"You think your mom would let me crash on the couch here for a few days?" he asked.

"No," Destini answered. Mom wouldn't even like the idea of him sitting on her nice couch when he obviously had not bathed in a while.

"She's a coldhearted woman, your mother," he commented.

"No, she's not. You got a job or what?" Destini asked.

"Times are hard. Don't you read the papers? Who can find a job these days?" he asked, shaking his head.

"I know a lot of people who're working," Destini said.

"You're getting just like your mother, girl, coldhearted," Dad told her.

"Know what, Dad? I'm in a group at church, and we take foster kids for little outings and it's really nice. We went camping with them and stuff and it was fun. Aren't you proud of me for helping other people?" Destini asked.

"No," he sighed. "It's all a racket. The minister is trying to rope people in to join his church."

"No," Destini declared, "these kids are lonely and we're really helping them, Dad. They never have any fun. My special little friend is named Amber, and we got to be close. We're talking like sisters. We're going to the movies on Friday and I'm really looking forward to it."

"I've never trusted do-gooders," Dad said.

Destini looked at her father. He was in his middle forties but he looked older. He didn't smell good. It was sad to realize he didn't care for himself or for anybody else. He never asked Destini how she was doing at school. He never asked her if she had a boyfriend. He didn't seem to care. "Dad, how come you're not interested in me at all?" Destini asked.

The man turned from the TV and looked at Destini. "I never asked to be a father. That was your mother's idea," he replied.

"But you *are* my father," Destini asserted.

"When I won that money on the ponies, I told her to throw you some, didn't I?" he said.

"I got a boyfriend now, Dad. Would you like to hear about him?" Destini asked.

"Nope," he said.

"His name is Tyron Becker. He's really nice. He's a junior at Tubman too and he says I'm beautiful," Destini rattled on. "I'm really, really excited about having my first boyfriend."

"It's all a crock," Dad said.

"His father is a hardworking man, but he doesn't make much money," Destini went on. "They aren't well-to-do, but that's all right. I'm used to that."

"Is his father Tyree Becker?" Dad asked, perking up.

"I don't know, maybe," Destini said. "Do you know him?"

"Well, I know a Tyree Becker," Dad replied. "When I had that job cleaning up at the construction site, he worked there too. He didn't have one of the good jobs. Just hanging around doing cleanup like me. His wife brought him his lunch every day. He said she nagged him day and night, and then he'd beat her and she'd shut up for a while. He asked me if I ever had to beat my wife and I told him I don't believe in that, and anyway, if I ever tried to beat your mother she'd kill me first and I'd not blame her."

Destini looked at her father and wondered. Was Tyree Becker Tyron's father? It made Destini sad to think so. If he was, then maybe he was just joking about beating his wife. Destini felt so sorry for Tyron if he had to live in a family where there was violence like that. "Dad, maybe this man was joking and he didn't really beat his wife," Destini suggested. "Men make jokes about stuff like that sometimes."

"No," Dad responded. "I'd see signs of it when she'd come around with his lunch. She'd have black eyes and bruises on her arms and face. She was a wreck. It was none of my business, but there she'd be, bringing the slob his lunch—a skinny, ratty looking woman without much weight on her, and him fat as a pig. One time when he wasn't looking, I walked over and gave her one of those flyers, you know for the women's shelters for the abused. I told her if she ever wanted to get out of there, this might be a place to go, but she looked at me as if I was crazy and went scampering off to her busted up old car."

Destini remembered Tyron complaining about how heavy his father was. She felt a little sick. Poor Tyron. It had to be terrible to live in that house and watch his poor mother get beaten. How could he be in that situation and still function and be nice at school? Destini tried to imagine what it would be like to see Dad hurt Mom. She didn't think she could stand watching that happen. She would do something desperate.

"Well, you're sure she won't let me crash here just this night, huh?" Dad asked.

"Otherwise I got to go downtown and beg that priest who takes in homeless for a bed."

"Wait," Destini ordered him. She went to the blue sugar bowl where Mom kept about a hundred dollars in twenties for emergencies. She told Destini if she needed to, she could borrow twenty from the blue sugar bowl on the second pantry shelf behind the brown sugar. Destini withdrew a twenty and took it to her father. "Dad, you can have this," she said. "I hope it helps."

"It sure does," Dad responded with a smile. "Thank you, Destini. Listen, someday I will win very big on the ponies. My time is coming up. I been on a losing streak for long enough. Then I will come here and wave a lot of money under your mother's nose, and she will finally respect me. As for you, girl, even though I didn't want a daughter, or a son, or anybody else with my genes in them, I will remember you when I am rich."

"Thank you, Dad," Destini said. She wanted to hug him. After all, he *was* her father. She wanted to hug him but he smelled of perspiration. Still, he was her father and in spite of how little he did to fulfill that role, she felt something for him. So she went over to him, put her arms around him, and hugged him. "See ya, Daddy," she sighed.

He seemed thin when she put her arms around him. She was glad she did it.

He went out the door with nothing but a smile. He walked down the street toward the bus stop. Destini watched him, feeling an ache in her heart, a kind of hole that this man who was almost a stranger should be filling. After school sometimes, Alonee's father would pick her up and he'd have these pet names for her—"Alonee-dolly" or "Alonee-lah-dee." Sami's father would give Sami big smooches, and Sami claimed it embarrassed the life out of her. Destini was jealous.

"He was here, wasn't he" Mom remarked when she got home.

"How'd you know, Mom?" Destini asked.

"I smell him. My Lord, where's the air freshener? He was after money, wasn't he?" Mom asked.

"Sort of," Destini said.

"Was he drunk again?" Mom asked.

"No, he was sober. He was pretty nice, Mom. We had a nice talk," Destini commented. "I guess there are worse men."

"Yep," Mom said as she sprayed the house with orange-scented freshener. "This is good stuff."

They sat down to dinner, and Destini told her mother she was taking good notes in English and American history and doing all her math homework. "I'm going to bring my grades up, Mom. I know I can do it," she declared.

"You can," Mom encouraged her. "You can make something of yourself, girl. That's what girls need to do. Be somebody on their own and get to be adults and be able to take care of their own selves. Get a good job, and then if you're of a mind to, marry a decent man if there are any of them left. But first find your own place in the world."

Destini curled up in a chair in her room and read the story assigned in English. Then she opened her diary and read the poem Tyron had given her again. How could he be so romantic and sensitive if Tyree Becker was really his father? It didn't seem possible. It was an awesome tribute to him that he could thrive in that environment. Knowing what challenges he faced made Destini love Tyron even more. Her heart overflowed with pity for him. She imagined him watching helplessly while his father abused his poor mother. It had to be tearing him apart inside.

But what could he do? There were younger children in the family. How could he call in the law and break up the family? They were poor. What would his mother do? Where could she go? Those shelters for abused women were all right for temporary safety, but in the long run what does a poor, uneducated woman with children do alone in the world?

"Destini," Mom called from the kitchen. "You didn't give him any, did you?"

"What?" Destini answered. "What? Who?" She knew very well what and whom her mother was talking about.

Mom appeared in the doorway to Destini's room. "Girl, there is a twenty missing from the blue sugar bowl. I pray to God you didn't give that no good free-loader that twenty dollar bill." She stood there like an avenging angel.

"Oh Mom, I'm sorry," Destini replied, thinking fast. "I should have told you. We're all putting in twenty dollars to help the expenses for the foster kids' outings. You know, to pay for the camping supplies and the movie tickets and stuff."

Mom smiled. "Oh, well that's just fine. I want you to do your share, Destini. I don't begrudge those children a little fun. That's just fine, baby. The good Lord expects us to share with the truly needy, not with drunken freeloaders like your father." She turned and went back to the kitchen.

Destini flopped on the bed and stared at the ceiling. She felt guilty. She was a liar. She learned long ago in Sunday school that it was a sin to lie, but this was even worse. She had taken twenty dollars from the blue sugar bowl and then lied about it, pretended it was for the poor children.

Destini got up and went to the closet where she kept her secret bank in the stomach of an old teddy bear. She unzipped the bear's stomach and went into a little leather pouch containing her savings. Destini had been saving money for some time to buy some nice clothes for summer. She had forty dollars saved. She pulled out a ten and decided to donate it to the foster kids program. That would ease her conscience a little bit anyway.

Destini's cell phone rang. "Hi," she said.

"Hi beautiful, guess who?" Tyron asked.

"Oh Tyron! How are you? I've been thinking about you," Destini responded.

"Are you up for Friday night?" he asked. "You know that great movie we saw the other night—*Saw Town*? Well, there's a sequel and it's even better. It's showing Friday. After the movie we can go for pizza and it'll be a great night. What do you say, beautiful?"

Destini's heart raced in panic. She couldn't tell Tyron she had already made plans to spend Friday night with the foster kids. He'd never understand. He'd be hurt and maybe angry too. She had to somehow get out of the date with him without hurting him. Destini didn't even consider canceling the movie with the kids. She couldn't do that to Amber when Alonee said the little girl was so looking forward to seeing Destini again.

"Oh Tyron," Destini moaned, "I'd love to go out with you Friday night, but my grandma's sick up in LA, and Mom and I have to get her to the hospital Friday . . ."

115

To herself, Destini said, "I'm sorry, Grandma. I'm sorry. I know you've been dead for ten years and now I'm using you in a lie to get myself out of a date, but I couldn't think of anything else."

"Oh, well that's too bad." Tyron responded. "Good luck to your grandma. I'll see you later then, beautiful."

He didn't seem mad. He seemed to accept what Destini said. How could anybody be angry with someone helping a sick grandmother?

"I used a lie again—a big one," Destini thought miserably. "But what could I do?" Tyron would have been furious to be rejected over a date with the foster kids. He would have surely thought Destini did not care for him as much as he cared for her. She could not risk a relationship so precious to her. It's not that Destini wanted to lie—she just felt she had to.

# CHAPTER SEVEN

When Friday night came, Pastor Bromley picked Destini up at her house. Amber was already in the van. Alonee, Jaris, Kevin, Sami, and Derrick were there with their charges too. "You guys," Destini pleaded, "if anybody asks you later on, I didn't come tonight, okay? I mean I'm supposed to be somewhere else, so don't tell anybody at school I was with you guys tonight."

"Uh-oh!" Jaris laughed. "This girl is balancing a crowded social life. Don't worry, Destini. None of us see you. There's a big blank space right where you're sitting, right Amber? You don't see Destini, do you?"

"Nope," Amber giggled, "I don't see her nowhere!"

The others joined in. Kevin asked, "Destini? Where is she?" Sami and Alonee chimed in too.

"I'm so glad you came," Amber told Destini. "There's something I need to ask you."

"Okay," Destini said. "Shoot."

"Well, you know this big ugly scar I got on my forehead?" Amber began.

"Yeah," Destini said. "Like these big ugly pimples I get on my forehead and my chin and my nose!"

Amber giggled. "No really. Something I got to ask you. My friend at school, she says I should wear my hair in bangs, real low bangs that come down and cover the scar. She says I ought to do that till the doctor maybe can fix the scar so it don't show so much," Amber said. "What do you think, Destini?"

"Nope," Destini answered. "When I first met you, I noticed the scar, but now I hardly see it. I'd just wear my hair the way I like it, and who cares about the scar?

You got such beautiful big eyes that everybody is gonna look at them first anyway."

Amber reached over and gave Destini a hug. "That's what I think too, but I was scared you'd side with my friend. I don't need to hide my old scar. You're awesome, Destini. I'm so glad we're friends."

"I got cream I put over my pimples so they don't stand out so much, Amber," Destini advised, reaching in her purse for the tube. "Our skin color is about the same. Just dab some of this on and the scar will sort of fade like my pimples."

Destini loved the seagull movie. Amber and the other kids squealed with joy at the special effects. The great white birds seemed to be flying over their heads in the theater, as the audience laughed and gasped. Afterward, they stopped for ice cream sundaes.

"I'm glad you're my big sister," Amber said as Destini started to get out of the van at her house. "Can I give you a hug?"

"You bet," Destini replied. "I'm glad you're my little sister. I always wanted a little sister like you."

Destini hurried up the walk to her door, and when she got inside, she noticed her mother's lights were out. Destini smiled to herself. Mom had assured Destini that she wouldn't wait up for her. Destini was perfectly safe with the church group. But in the end Mom couldn't stop being a mom.

Destini went to bed happy. She hugged her pillow and relived the wonderful evening. She was so glad she went. She couldn't remember being this happy in a long time. She'd bonded with Alonee and Sami like she had not done before. She enjoyed hanging with the boys too, without worrying about what Tyron would say, and she especially enjoyed the kids.

Destini didn't hear from Tyron over the rest of the weekend. But on Monday morning, soon after she arrived at school, Tyron walked up to her. "How's your grandmother? Did she get to the hospital okay?" he asked. "It must have been hard for you and your mom to drive way up there in all the weekend traffic."

"Yeah, everything went well. Thanks for asking, Tyron," Destini replied, but she felt strange. There was something troubling in the expression on Tyron's face. He looked tense. He didn't look like himself. He was not smiling, but a strange, disturbing grimace turned the corners of his mouth.

"So what was wrong with your grandmother?" Tyron asked. He was nervously twirling his watch on his wrist, turning the silver band around and around in a frenzied way.

Destini felt a creeping, numb sensation moving through her body. "Uh . . . heart problems. She's, uh, had them for a long time . . . she had a pacemaker put in," Destini answered. Her mouth was going dry.

Grandma did have heart problems. That part was true. She had a pacemaker too. Grandma was seventy when she died of a massive heart attack.

"She live alone?" Tyron persisted. "That's kind of dangerous. An old lady with heart problems living alone. Maybe she could move down here with you and your mom. Then you could look after her better." Tyron's half smile disappeared entirely. His face looked cold and rigid.

"Maybe," Destini responded. She was frightened. Did he know something? Was he toying with her? Had somebody in the van betrayed her? She couldn't imagine any of her friends doing that.

"So, was the traffic bad going up there?" he asked again. "Friday nights are usually pretty heavy . . . "

"It was okay," Destini said.

"So, how about after school today we go over and have some more of those good egg rolls? Remember how you liked them, babe?" Tyron suggested. His lower lip trembled.

"Oh, that'd be great," Destini said, hoping against hope that everything was all right and that her imagination was just working overtime. Maybe there was trouble in Tyron's house and that was why he was acting so stressed. If there had been more violence, naturally he wouldn't be himself.

After her last class that day, Destini hurried to meet Tyron in the school parking lot. Bennie was there, waiting in the old Chevrolet. Tyron leaned against the car, drumming his fingers in his open hand.

Destini climbed in the back seat with Tyron and Bennie said, "Here we go."

But they didn't turn at the intersection that led to the fish restaurant where they had had the egg rolls. They turned in another direction, down a narrow, tree-lined street that fronted on a park. Bennie slowed down and then pulled onto the shoulder of the road. Bennie got out of the driver's seat and started walking down the road. Before he got more than a few feet, he said, "See you in about thirty minutes." Then he walked on.

"We need to talk," Tyron insisted.

123

Destini felt sick. For a minute she thought she might faint. All day she had been hoping and praying that everything was all right. Now she knew with a dreadful certainty that things were not all right.

"Babe, why did you lie to me?" Tyron asked bluntly.

"What do you mean?" Destini asked him.

"You wanted to be with that dude Derrick Shaw, right? That's why you blew me off, right?" Tyron asked bitterly.

"Tyron," Destini cried, "what are you talking about? You're talking crazy. I don't care one bit for Derrick. I care about you."

"If you really loved me, babe, you would have gone to the movies with me on Friday night. Instead you went to the movies with Derrick Shaw. And you made up that lie about a sick grandmother to cover it up. Jasmine saw you and Shaw getting popcorn at the movie theater," Tyron declared.

Destini started to cry. "Oh Tyron," she sobbed, "I'm so sorry that I lied to you.

I know that was wrong. I didn't want to hurt your feelings when you called for a date. I'd promised those foster kids to go to the movies with them, and I knew if I told you the truth you'd think I was choosing them over you, but I wasn't! On the spur of the moment I lied, Tyron. I'm so sorry. But it has nothing to do with Derrick Shaw. It was mainly because of this one little girl— Amber. She had her heart set on me being there and I couldn't cancel it."

"More lies," Tyron snarled. "Jasmine said you and Derrick looked real cozy buying that popcorn."

"Tyron, I swear, the only reason I went to the movies on Friday night with the foster kids and not with you was because of this little girl, Amber. She's so vulnerable—" Destini was about to explain about Amber's scar and all she had been through, but she never got the chance to finish her sentence.

Tyron's hand came up and slammed against Destini's mouth in a stinging blow that made her lip bleed. Destini gasped and began to sob. Her shoulders convulsed as she cried, and the blood ran down her chin and onto her pale blue sweater.

Tyron looked horrified. He pulled a handkerchief from his pocket and tried to stem the blood from Destini's lip. "I'm sorry, babe, I didn't mean to do that," he stammered, beginning to shake. "I'm sorry—I'm sorry. I just can't stand the thought of losing you, of you betraying me." He pulled out a second handkerchief and this time stopped the blood flowing from Destini's lip.

Tyron took Destini into his arms and stroked her head. He was crying now. As he held her, he was shaking with sobs too. "I'm sorry. I never meant to hurt you. I love you so much. Please forgive me. I love you so much. I didn't mean it . . . I didn't mean it . . . "

Destini looked into Tyron's face. Tears streamed from his eyes down his cheeks. His lips quivered. "I'm sorry, babe," he said. "I'll make it up to you, I swear I will.

I'll never hurt you again. I swear on my life I'll never hurt you again."

"I just went to the movies for the kids," Destini whispered. "There was nothing else . . . "

"I know, I know," Tyron said. "I don't know what got into me. I'm so sorry. Are you okay?"

"Yes, I'm okay," Destini replied. Her lips tasted salty from the blood. She got out her compact mirror and saw the nasty bruise and cut on her lower lip. But it had stopped bleeding.

"Will you forgive me, Destini? Please, please say you'll forgive me," Tyron urged.

"I forgive you," Destini said.

Tyron took her in his arms again and stroked her head and her back. His hands moved gently through her hair, along her shoulders. "I love you. I love you so much," he told her. "Nothing like this will ever happen again, ever. I swear on my life that it won't."

"Okay," Destini said. "I believe you . . . I guess we better . . . you know . . . go home."

"You've really forgiven me?" he asked.

"Yes," Destini answered.

Bennie returned to the car. He did a double take on Destini. He swore under his breath, then he got behind the wheel and drove.

"Take her home, man," Tyron told his brother. "I lost it. I could kick myself across the county. I lost it, man. Ohhh!" He seemed genuinely grief stricken.

From the front Bennie advised, "It's not bad, sweetheart. It'll heal quick. Just tell your mom you slipped and cut your lip on a fence or something."

Destini said nothing. All the way to the house she said nothing. Her mind was whirling like a windmill. As the car stopped at her house, Tyron was agitated. "Baby, I'll make it up to you. You'll see. I'll do something so wonderful that you'll forget this day, okay?"

"Okay," Destini agreed.

As the car pulled away, Destini walked slowly to her house. Her mother was in the living room. She turned and looked at Destini. "Honey, what happened to your lip?" she asked.

"I . . . I stumbled on that stupid fence at school and I cut it. It's not bad though. Tyron's brother drove me home so I wouldn't have to take the bus," Destini explained.

"I'll put some benzoic acid and camphor on it, baby, and it'll be fine," Mom assured her. "Nice of those boys to bring you home."

Destini went to her bedroom after her mother doctored her. Her lip didn't hurt anymore. She lay down on her bed and started to cry.

How could he have hit her like that? He said he loved her. How could he have hit her? But she had lied to him. She never should have done that. How would she feel if Tyron had made up a story to cancel a date with her, and then she found out he was out having fun, maybe with someone else? Destini knew she would have been

129

devastated too. It was so wrong of her to lie like that. She should have had the courage to tell Tyron she had promised to be with the kids Friday night. He might have gotten upset, but it would not have been as bad as a lie. It wouldn't have come to this.

"He got so mad because he loves me," Destini thought. "If he didn't really love me, he wouldn't have cared if I was out with somebody else. That proves he loves me. But he hit me! He struck me. He cut my lip and made a big bruise. Mom said there was a special place in hell for men who hurt women and children" she agonized.

"But Tyron did not mean to do that. It was almost like an accident. He was just wild with fear that he was losing me. He was so sorry at once. He was crying. He was really crying. He was grief stricken over what he had done." Destini got up slowly and went to her diary. She reread the poem Tyron had given her.

She is lovely as a rose, she is my dearest treasure,

She is the one I chose, loved beyond all measure,

I thank the fates that brought us together.

Destini clutched the poem to her chest. She had never been loved like that by a boy. That love had transformed her life. She felt so sad and lonely before Tyron came into her life, and now he made her feel lifted up and happy. Everything was beautiful since she met Tyron. The air itself had a fragrance that she never noticed before. Everything was different and brighter.

Tyron made a mistake. He made a terrible mistake. But so did Destini. She lied to him. She must never lie again. She must be honest with Tyron. Their relationship must be built on truth.

"I'll never lie to him again, never," Destini resolved. "Then everything will be all right. It'll be as it was before. He'll never hurt me again. Never." Lying was something Destini had control over. All she had to do was be honest . . .

It dawned on Destini that Jasmine had done a very evil thing by telling Tyron that she saw Destini at the movies and that Derrick Shaw was there too. Why would she do such a thing? Why didn't she come to Destini and ask her why she was at the movies with other people instead of with Tyron? Destini could have explained herself.

Jasmine was the real culprit in all this, not Tyron. She had caused the whole thing, and Destini hated her because of it. Destini felt like going to her and smudging her hideous green eye shadow and telling her she looked like a witch—and she *was* a witch.

But Destini couldn't do that. Jasmine was Marko's girl, and Tyron thought everything Marko did was perfect, including his choice of Jasmine. So Destini had to be nice to Jasmine even though she hated her. It made Destini sick, but that's the way it was.

# CHAPTER EIGHT

At school on Tuesday morning, Destini made a big deal out of telling everyone how she had stumbled and fallen into the school fence and cut her lip. She called herself a clumsy oaf. She laughed about it. She made jokes about it. She didn't want anybody to suspect for a minute what really happened.

When Destini saw Tyron, she smiled at him as if nothing had happened. He looked at her nervously. He leaned close and whispered, "After school, meet me by Harriet Tubman's statue. I got something for you. I got something to prove how much I love you."

Destini smiled at him and headed for her first class. On the way she met Alonee

Lennox. The two girls looked at one another. Alonee grabbed Destini's hand, "Girl, you okay?"

"I'm fine, I'm great," Destini replied.

"For sure?" Alonee asked, "because . . ."

"I couldn't be better," Destini cried almost fiercely, rushing for her English class.

All day Destini struggled to concentrate on her classes and to appear normal. Inside her mind there was turmoil. She would be angry and hurt one minute and then blame in all on herself the next. Once or twice she even considered breaking up with Tyron. She would tell him that what had happened had changed everything and it couldn't be fixed. But the thought of doing that filled her with a desperate loneliness. And then she quickly made excuses for him again.

Destini had come to love Tyron. There was no getting around that. At first it was just the thought of having a boyfriend, but now it was more. Every time she thought of him, her heart stirred. She had begun looking forward to seeing him as the highlight of the day. At night she dreamed about him. He was the first person she thought of in the morning when she woke up and the last person she thought of before going to sleep at night.

When the last bell of the day rung, Destini walked to the statue of Harriet Tubman. She sat on the grass there and pretended to be reading her American history textbook.

Maybe he wouldn't come, she thought. Maybe he wouldn't show up at all. Tyron had been so emotional about the whole thing. Maybe now he was ashamed to face her. Maybe the incident had damaged him even more than it damaged her.

The flow of students going by quickly thinned out. Only a few passed by now. A few said "Hi" to Destini. She looked up briefly from her book as if she were very intent on reading it. She glanced at her watch. If he didn't come soon, she would miss the regular bus and have a long wait for the next one.

And then the shadow of a boy fell across the page of Destini's book. "Tyron," she breathed, looking up at him and smiling. It hurt her lip when she smiled, but she did it anyway.

Tyron reached down and took Destini's hand, pulling her gently to her feet. "Want to go across the street to the pizza place?" he asked. "Don't worry about being late getting home. Bennie will drive you."

"Okay," Destini agreed.

They walked across the street and Destini decided against pizza. The chewing would only start her lip bleeding again. She ordered a mocha, and they sat in a little alcove. The place was not busy now but later on it would fill up fast.

Tyron took a box out of his pocket. It was not large, about the size of a cell phone. He put the box on the table between them.

Destini looked at the box. "For me?" she asked.

"You bet. Nothing but the best for the best," he said. "Open it up, beautiful."

Destini's hands were shaking as she opened the box. She gasped at the sight of the gold chain curled up on a bed of cotton. The chain held a heart-shaped pendant with the word *Love* in the center. It was the most beautiful thing Destini had ever seen. "Ohhh Tyron, it's real gold, isn't it?" she breathed.

"Yeah, you think I wouldn't get you gold?" he exclaimed. "Try it on."

Destini tried to clasp the chain around her neck but she was fumbling with it. Tyron took it and put it around her neck with the little heart at her throat. "Just wait till you're wearing a nice vee-necked dress, babe. That necklace will really stand out. You'll be the envy of every chick at Tubman."

Destini looked at the gold chain in her compact mirror. "Oooo," she gasped. "It looks so beautiful!" Then she felt sad thinking he couldn't have afforded such a thing. "Tyron, it must have cost a fortune . . ."

"Marko helped me out. Marko always helps me out. He knows how much you mean to me, babe. If I could have given you a real star from the sky, I woulda ridden on

137

one of those spaceships and pulled it down. I want to prove to you how much I love you. I'll never get mad at you again, babe . . . not like I did. Never. I swear. You believe me, don't you?" Tyron's voice was high-pitched and shaky.

"I believe you, Tyron," Destini sighed. "Oh, this is so beautiful. I never thought I'd ever have something like this in my entire life. I feel like a movie star or something. I feel like a princess." Destini threw her arms around Tyron and kissed him. "I love you!" she cried. "Thank you for the most beautiful gift in the world."

When Bennie dropped Destini off at her home, she had made up her mind not to mention the gift to her mother. Mom wouldn't understand how a junior in high school could give Destini such an expensive gift. So Destini went into her bedroom and opened the bottom drawer of her dresser. She had a little ivory box there with a lock. Inside was her diary, and now she slid the jewel box in beside it.

One of these days, Destini thought, she would buy a really lovely dress and go on a date with Tyron and wear the gold chain with its pendant and feel like Cinderella at the ball. None of the girls at Tubman had such a piece of jewelry, except maybe Jasmine. Destini had envied them for their boyfriends and their beauty and popularity. Now they could envy her. They would see that Destini had a boyfriend who treasured her so much he would buy her a gold chain.

At school the next morning, Marko and Jasmine met Destini on her way in. "Hey Destini, how's it going?" Marko asked. Jasmine didn't say anything. Destini figured she knew she had done a rotten thing ratting Destini out. Destini wondered if she knew what a terrible incident she had caused.

"It's going great," Destini replied. "I'm ready for the history test. I really studied. I got a C plus going in history, and I think I can bring it up to a B."

"How do you like your bling, girl?" Marko asked. Apparently he knew about

Tyron's gift. Tyron said as much—Marko helped him get it.

"It's so beautiful. I love it," Destini said.

"You know what it means, don't you?" Marko asked.

"Well sure. It means, Tyron really cares about me," Destini answered.

"That too," Marko agreed, "but it also means that there is a little invisible stamp on you, girl. It says 'Property of Tyron Becker. Do not touch.' Nobody can see the stamp, but it's there. You know it's there."

Destini didn't know quite what to say. Jasmine finally spoke up. "Means no cheatin', girl. No double dealin'. That's what it means."

Destini glared at Jasmine. "I'd never cheat on Tyron, not ever," she snapped.

"See that you don't," Marko advised. "You are one lucky girl, little sister. Tyron is my main man and you got a winner there. He's on the football team, he's got a lot of friends, and he picked you. No offense girl, but you're not exactly the hottest chick on campus, yet he picked you. You got to appreciate that." Marko walked off then with Jasmine hanging on his arm.

Destini felt insulted. At this moment she hated Marko Lane almost as much as she hated Jasmine. Marko acted as if Destini wasn't worth much and Tyron was doing her a big favor by dating her. But Marko was Tyron's best friend, so Destini made up her mind to just ignore what he said.

The American history test was in two parts, multiple choice and two essays. Usually upon seeing such a test, Destini would have groaned in despair, but she had prepared. There were a lot of details about the Jimmy Carter administration and the first term of President Ronald Reagan. Destini felt good about her multiple-choice answers. One essay asked about the Iran hostage crisis and its root causes. Destini had read the chapter in the book about it, plus she went on the Internet for more information. Now she wrote a pretty good essay. The second essay asked about Reagan's appeal in the 1980 election. Destini did well on that too. Most of the test looked familiar to her because she was ready for it.

When it was time to turn in the test, Destini didn't have the usual queasy feeling in her stomach. She wasn't fearful of having flunked the test. She was just hoping for a B, maybe even a B plus.

On Saturday, Destini and her mother went shopping at the local supermarket. As they pulled into the parking lot, Destini recognized Bennie Becker's old Chevrolet parked there already. You couldn't miss it. Both front fenders were mashed in. Destini thought the Becker family might be here doing their shopping for the week too.

Destini didn't see Bennie or Tyron in the market as she shopped with her mother. It was a big store and they could easily have been in another part of it. When Destini and her mother were checking out, Mom said, "I got to go to the dollar store next door, baby. You put the groceries in the car and I'll be there in ten minutes. I got to pick up a few things."

Destini took the car keys and pushed the shopping cart into the parking lot. She unloaded all the groceries into the trunk and glanced over at the Becker Chevrolet still parked. Then she saw them, a heavy man and a slender woman coming from the store with their shopping cart. There was a lot of stuff in the cart, and the woman pushed it by herself. When they got to the car, the man opened the trunk, got into the front seat of the car, and sat there. Mrs. Becker began unloading heavy jugs of orange juice and milk. She lifted several twelve-can cartons of soda into the trunk and almost dropped one of them. She had to put some of the stuff in the back seat of the car. She seemed to stagger as she stuffed the bags through the door, as if she were exhausted.

Mr. Becker had turned on the car radio, and he was drumming his fingers to some rap music. Once he looked back and said something to his wife. Destini couldn't hear what he said, but the wife said, "I'm hurrying."

Finally Mrs. Becker had finished unloading the cart, and she looked around for a safe place to place the empty cart. She began walking toward a cart corral. Mr. Becker saw her pushing the empty cart and screamed, "Just leave the freakin' cart and come on!"

Mrs. Becker abandoned the cart in the middle of the parking lot and ran to the car. The cart went rattling across the lot, almost hitting a parked car. Mrs. Becker's feet were barely in the Chevrolet when her husband started it up and roared off.

Destini felt sick. Poor Tyron, she thought again. His father didn't seem to be a very nice man. He should have helped his wife unload the groceries. Now, at home, the poor thing would probably have to unload them again and put them away.

Mom came from the dollar store with a bag. She was smiling. "I got a lot of little things, all for under ten bucks. I just love that store."

On the way home, Destini asked, "Mom, you don't know the Becker family, do you?"

"That your boyfriend's family?" Mom inquired. "No, I don't know them. I'm not a gadabout like some women. I got too much work to do to go nosing into other peoples' business. Sometimes I wish I could just sit down and drink coffee and yak with the other women, but it ain't happenin' anytime soon. How come you ask, Destini?"

"Oh, I just wondered," Destini responded. "They work hard, but they don't have much money."

"Join the club," Mom sighed. "One thing this 'hood ain't big on, and that's rich folks."

After Destini and her mother unloaded all the groceries into the house, Destini went to her room to admire the gold chain

145

Tyron had given her. She trembled at the beauty of it, gently touching the shining links with her fingertips. Then Destini checked her teddy bear bank. She had thirty dollars. If Mom would put a little more to that, Destini could get a really nice dress, and she could wear the gold chain with it. Tyron would be so proud of her.

On Monday, Ms. McDowell returned the history tests. "Some of you did quite well and others left much to be desired," the teacher said as she handed out the tests. Destini glimpsed at Marko's grade—C plus. Marko looked disappointed. He often made Bs in history.

Destini was eager to see her grade. She was really hoping for a B. When Ms. McDowell put the test down on her desk, Destini let out a little gasp. It was an A minus. Destini had not gotten an A in anything since middle school. Ms. McDowell wrote on the paper, "Good work. I knew you could do it!"

As the students milled around after class, Destini said, "Oh wow, I got an A!"

Jaris smiled at her. "Good for you. I got a B minus," he replied.

Destini couldn't wait for lunch to tell Tyron her good news. Getting that A was really a big deal for her. When Destini saw Tyron at the beverage machine, she rushed over. "Tyron! I just got an A in history!" she cried happily. "Is that amazing or what?"

Marko was standing beside Tyron and he said, "Old McDowell, she prefers chicks. She hates guys, you know. She's one of the freaky man-hating women who like to screw guys over. She gave me a lousy, freakin' C!"

"That's too bad, Marko," Tyron said, ignoring Destini's good news. "It's really unfair when a teacher sides with chicks and messes up a guy's grades."

Destini was disappointed. She wanted Tyron to share in her happiness over her A. But all Tyron and Marko wanted to talk about was how unfair Ms. McDowell was in her grading.

Derrick Shaw came along with a smile on his face. As much as Marko abused Derrick, he didn't bear grudges. Marko hailed him, "Hey Shaw, you flunk history? I got a C, so I figure you probably got an F!"

"No," Derrick said, "I got a C too. C plus. I'm happy with that."

Marko looked shocked. He said out loud, "That weirdo got a C plus and I got the same grade? What's going down here?"

Alonee heard the commotion and joined the little knot of students around the beverage machine. When she heard about Destini's A, she gave her a hug. "Way to go, girl," she said. Then Alonee turned to Marko. "You got a C? Lemme see your test." Alonee began to laugh as she read Marko's essay. "You big goof— listen—you write that the root cause of the Iran hostage crisis was that Saddam Hussein was mad at the United States. He was from Iraq! You're lucky McDowell didn't flunk you!"

"Stop laughing at me, you little witch," Marko snapped. "You side with McDowell because you hate guys too. That's why nobody wants to go out with you except that fool Trevor Jenkins."

"Oh Marko," Alonee blew him off, "why don't you crawl back into the woodwork where all the good little insects are?" She laughed and walked away.

Destini kept looking at Tyron, waiting for him to say something about her A. She thought at least he'd tell her he was a little proud of her. But he didn't say anything until Marko walked away. Then he turned to Destini and said, "Do you still like the gold chain I gave you, or are you tired of it?"

"Oh Tyron, I love it. I'll always love it," Destini told him.

"Destini, let's go to a party Friday night. Marko's dad is having a party at a classy club. You can wear a nice dress and the gold chain, okay?" Tyron asked.

"Okay, Tyron," Destini responded. "I'll buy a dress just for the party. What color do you like?"

"Yellow," Tyron said. "You'll be a knockout in yellow, babe. Make it sleeveless with a vee neck, okay? Above the knees, right? Oh baby, every guy there will look at you and eat his heart out. They can look but they better not touch, 'cause you're mine!" He laughed and said, "I can't wait to see that gold chain around your beautiful little neck!"

Destini laughed too. Tyron seemed so happy with her. And she was so happy now with him, and with her success in American history, and with everything. To top it all off, she was going shopping for a yellow dress.

# CHAPTER NINE

After school, Destini rushed home to tell her mother of her special need for a dress.

"I'm going to this really nice party where all the girls will have really great dresses, Mom, and I so want to look extra nice and I need to wear something special," Destini blurted.

"Go look in your closet, baby," Mom advised. "Plenty nice dresses there. If something needs to be cleaned or pressed, we can do that. We got no money for fru-fru dresses like those movie stars wear. I'm saving every extra penny I make for your college. That's what important child."

Destini thought that now was the time to spring her good news on her mother.

"Mom, I studied and studied and read and went on the Internet and everything. And you know what? Ms. McDowell gave the tests in American history back today and I got an A!"

Mom stopped in her tracks. She spun around. "Get outta here," she cried. "No way you made an A in American history or in anything else, girl. You ain't done that since you were twelve years old!"

Destini giggled and pulled the test from her binder. "Look what Ms. McDowell wrote, Mom. See, right by the A!" Destini pointed out her teacher's comment.

Mom's eyes got as big as supersized ginger snaps and she shouted, "Praise the Lord. I didn't think I would live to see the day when you got an A, child. Destini Fletcher, you have made me a proud and happy woman!"

"So . . ." Destini went on, "about the dress. I saw dresses in the Sunday paper at Lawson's on sale and they're marked down to thirty-six dollars and I've got thirty dollars saved, Mom, so maybe if you'd give me a little bit more. Oh Mom, I so want a yellow dress and I don't have any yellow dresses. I'll get a lot of wear out of it. Please Mom? We could go now and look at Lawson's racks. If we wait any longer all the nice dresses will be gone."

"Ohhh, all right," Mom relented. "Come on, I guess you getting an A in American history calls for a celebration — and a new dress."

"Oh Mom, thank-you-thank-you-thank-you," Destini chanted, racing to get her thirty dollars from her teddy bear pouch.

Not much later, at Lawson's, Destini flew into the store ahead of her mother, heading for the sale racks. She saw a lot of dresses she would have liked, but Tyron wanted her to wear a yellow dress and she would not settle for less. Destini hurried from rack to rack, and then she saw it. She held her breath to see if it was the right size. "Size 6, Mom. This cute dress is size 6!" Destini squealed. "It's got a vee neck and it's sleeveless, Mom. Isn't this an amazing dress?"

"It's too short," Mom complained.

"No, it's not," Destini protested, remembering that Tyron wanted it above her knees. "I'm gonna try it on, Mom. Where's the dressing room?"

"Right over here," Mom said, leading the way. They went inside a tiny dressing room and Mom sat on the narrow bench. Destini wiggled out of her jeans and tank top and climbed into the yellow dress. It fit her perfectly. It hugged her tiny waist and swirled around her legs. "Mom, it's so beautiful! Oh, I love it. Don't you love it, Mom?"

"No, I don't love it," Mom declared, "but I love you, girl, and I do admit you look very pretty in the dress, so you can have it if you want it."

When Destini got home she tried on the dress again, and this time she put on the gold chain and locket. The effect was stunning. Destini was so happy she felt like running outside and dancing down the street to tell everybody she was the luckiest girl in the world.

Friday night finally came, and Bennie picked up Destini at six-thirty. He told her Tyron was already at the party waiting for her. "He gonna freak when he sees you, little girl," Bennie commented with a smile.

They drove down to a beach restaurant with a view of the ocean. It was closed for a private party. The occasion was Marko's father's fortieth birthday, and he had invited all his friends as well as Marko's. There was a good-sized dance floor and a recognized band that was already on the hip-hop charts.

Most of the cars in the parking lot were expensive. The old Chevrolet looked out of place. Destini walked in with Bennie, and she immediately spotted Tyron and Marko standing with a tall, handsome man in a silk Italian-made suit. He wore many golden chains.

"Destini," Tyron called out. "Babe, you're a vision! My golden angel. Come and meet Marko's dad." Destini hurried over to be greeted by the tall, smiling man. "Well," he grinned, "so this is the little sister you've been telling us about, Tyron. She is most lovely."

"Thank you," Destini replied.

"This is Chuck Lane, my dad," Marko said with obvious pride. "This is the man."

Chuck Lane was handsome enough to grace the covers of any fine man's magazine. Destini thought he probably did. He had deep, dark brown eyes and classic features, and Destini could see where Marko got his good looks. "So, Destini," the man said, "you go to Tubman High with my son."

"Yes, we're in a lot of the same classes," Destini answered.

"Delighted to meet you," Marko's father said and moved toward a cluster of newly arrived guests. Destini didn't recognize most of the people in the place. They seemed to be in their twenties or thirties.

There were some beautiful women in stunning dresses. And Jasmine appeared wearing a beautiful red dress. She also wore gold chains.

Destini was glad when Tyron led her off to a little corner where they sat down. There was a spectacular view of the ocean from a nearby window. "Tyron, is Marko's mother here?" Destini asked. The moment she asked the question, she felt foolish. None of the women looked like they might run a house-cleaning service.

Tyron laughed a little. "No, she couldn't make it," he said. Then he added, "Babe, Marko's parents travel in two different worlds."

"Who are all these people?" Destini inquired.

"Marko's father's friends. Business associates. He runs a modeling agency. Those are some of the girls. And he's into indie movies," Tyron explained.

"I guess we're the only ones from Tubman except for Jasmine," Destini commented.

Tyron laughed again. "Babe, you are so funny," he chuckled.

Outside the restaurant was a little tiled patio. The moon was overhead, peeking through the royal palm trees. Tyron led Destini out there and took her in his arms, and they danced. A man was playing the piano inside between the hip-hop sets.

"Tyron, don't you feel funny here?" Destini asked him.

"Yeah, sure," Tyron replied. "But it's Marko's father's world. All the good stuff Marko has and what he does for me. This is where it comes from." He laughed in a strange, bitter way. "I can imagine my old man stepping in this place. It'd be like a wild boar in a castle. My old man would think he'd been captured by aliens and brought to a strange planet."

"I suppose your father does the best he can," Destini suggested.

Tyron didn't answer right away. Then he said, "I don't want to be like him. Like my father, I mean. I want to be like Marko's father. Look at him. Look how everybody kisses up to him. Like Marko says, he's the man . . . "

"What exactly does Marko's dad do?" Destini asked.

"He charms the world, babe," Tyron said. "He makes stuff happen."

But Destini wanted to know what he did for a living, other than running the model agency and the vague indie business. What did all these well dressed men and women have to do with Marko's father? Did they give him money? For what?

"I don't ask questions, babe," was all Tyron would say. And that was the end of it.

They went inside and had a fabulous dinner: white fish and chicken spiced up with cayenne peppers. It was Tunisian food. Destini had never tasted it before but she liked it. One of the waiters said Tunisian hot sauce, *harissa*, was hotter than the Moroccan version. Destini liked the dinner, but more than anything she liked dancing with Tyron, being in his arms and feeling close to him.

"Your dress is fantastic," Tyron whispered. "It's just what I hoped for. You're my angel, babe. Do you still like the gold chain? It looks perfect with the dress."

"I will always love the gold chain because it's from you, Tyron," Destini cooed.

It was a strangely beautiful evening, but it was unreal. Destini did not feel at home here. She was relieved when the evening ended, she got into the old Chevrolet with Tyron and Bennie, and headed for home. Bennie drove as usual, and Tyron and Destini sat in the back. Tyron put his arm around Destini's shoulders and pulled her close to him and they snuggled.

"I can't believe you're mine, babe," Tyron remarked.

Destini remembered what Marko had said the other day. That there's "a little invisible stamp on you, girl. It says 'Property of Tyron Becker. Do not touch.' " Something about that scared Destini, but she quickly put it out of her mind. It was such a warm and comfortable feeling to be with Tyron that she refused to let anything spoil it.

"I hate for tonight to end, Destini," Tyron said as they neared her house. "I'd like to be with you all night and tomorrow and forever."

"Yeah, but I promised Mom I'd be home by eleven," Destini replied.

"I know," Tyron said. "I'm just dreaming, babe."

They pulled into Destini's driveway and she started to get out of the car. Tyron took her hand and pulled her toward him. He kissed her on the lips. He held her in his arms and wouldn't let go. "I love you so much," he whispered.

"Me too," Destini sighed, kissing him back. Finally he let her out of the car. Destini walked to her door, stopped and turned around, blowing Tyron another kiss. Her lip was all healed now. She didn't even think about what happened anymore. But now, because Tyron had kissed her so hard, her lip hurt a little where it had healed. But Destini didn't mind.

At school on Monday, Sami met Destini as she walked from the bus. "Destini," Sami called out, "you look so pretty girl. You are blossoming."

"Thanks Sami," Destini called back.

A boy was standing there, a boy Destini had seen many times on the bus. Once she hoped he'd stop to talk to her, but he never did. Now he was looking at her.

"Hi," he said. "Aren't we in Buckingham's science class."

"Yeah," Destini answered.

"I'm Quincy Pierce," he went on. "My mom works at the same hospital your mom works at. You're Destini, right? Mom said to say hello to you. She really likes your mom."

"Oh yeah," Destini replied. "She talks about Suzy Pierce all the time. She likes her too."

Destini was suddenly nervous. She was standing in front of Harriet Tubman's statue chatting with a cute boy. Was anyone spying on her? She glanced around, expecting Jasmine to be hiding behind the statue, but she wasn't. Destini breathed a sigh of relief, but she said no more to Quincy Pierce. It was unlike her to be cold and unfriendly to a classmate, but she was a little bit afraid.

As she walked to class, Destini thought about Sereeta and Jaris being friends, but they were free to chat with other people. Kevin and Carissa were close, but they had other friends. But, Destini thought, poor Tyron was insecure. That's why Destini had to be extra careful not to hurt his feelings.

When Destini got home from school, she learned that Mom had left work early to help Dad. Her mother was putting some soup and a salad in containers. "Honeychild, your father called. He's feeling poorly, so I'm taking him some supper. His brother, Anson, has been letting him stay in that empty house Anson is trying to sell, but your father is just laying around trying to live on potato chips and beer!"

Destini knew that, as angry and disgusted as Mom was with Dad, she still, deep down, cared a little for him. She made him some pea soup with ham and a nice salad with tomatoes and greens.

They drove to the empty house and found Destini's father lying on a recliner watching television.

"We brought you some dinner," Mom announced in a businesslike voice. "You been neglecting your health."

"Smells tolerable," Dad commented. He winked at Destini.

"The salad is real good, Dad," Destini said. "It's got that creamy dressing that you like."

When they were getting ready to leave, Destini dashed over and planted a kiss on her father's unshaven cheek.

"At least the poor child loves me," Dad declared.

"Little you've done to deserve it, mister," Mom told him. Then she added, "If you need anything, you got our phone number. Don't be drinking anymore tonight. You drank enough. I see beer bottles all over the place. Eat the soup and salad." As they walked through the darkness to the car, Mom turned to Destini and said, "He looks bad."

# CHAPTER TEN

$O$n the ride home, Mom said, "Fool of a man, he's let his whole life go down the drain. When his time comes, who's gonna bury him? He probably doesn't have no burial insurance. So you know what that means?"

It made Destini sad to think of her father dying. He never was much of a father, but in some way she did love him. "What does it mean, Mom?"

"Means they put him in a pauper's grave. Like an animal. County does it. Regular burials cost money. So what do we do? Let him go to a pauper's grave or spend eight or nine thousand on a burial when that's more than we even got in the bank.

And I'm saving that for your college," Mom stated.

"Oh Mom," Destini said, "it wouldn't be right not to have a funeral in Pastor Bromley's church and a burial in the cemetery with his mom and pop . . ."

"Easy to say, child," Mom said, "but all these years I been putting away money for your future. For college. Should I cheat you for a man who never done right by us?"

"Mom, maybe Dad won't die real soon," Destini suggested. "Maybe he'll be okay and he won't die until I'm finished with school and I'm making money on a job. Then I'll, you know, take care of him, Mom."

"Maybe," Mom murmured, driving down the dark streets.

In science the next day, Quincy walked up to Destini's desk. "I'm sorry if I upset you yesterday," he apologized. "It's just that your mom and mine are such good friends."

Destini looked at the boy. He was really nice looking. She smiled at him. "Oh, you didn't upset me," she told him. "I just had something else on my mind. My mom always talks about having coffee at the breaks with your mom."

Quincy smiled with relief. "I was worried I'd scared you or something. You looked scared."

"Oh no," Destini said, laughing.

At lunch, Destini couldn't find Tyron, so she joined Alonee and Sami for lunch.

"Did you guys meet Quincy Pierce yet?" Alonee asked as she peeled her orange.

"Yeah, I met him," Destini responded. "His mom and mine work at the same hospital. They're good friends."

"Speak of the boy," Sami chimed in, "look at him over there wandering around like a lost soul. Hey, Quincy, over here. Join us for lunch."

Quincy grinned and walked slowly over. "Just bought some hot dogs for lunch," said. "They smell funny."

"Don't worry boy," Sami said, "you can always get your stomach pumped."

"Where you from, Quincy?" Alonee asked.

"Los Angeles. My mom got the job here and we moved down a few weeks ago," Quincy answered.

They were all talking and joking, when Destini had a strange feeling of fear. She turned sharply and saw Jasmine standing nearby, staring at her. Destini got up and walked over to Jasmine.

"He's a cute dude," Jasmine remarked. "Tyron sent me to tell you he's doing football practice and he's sorry he missed meeting you for lunch. But looks like you're doin' fine."

"Jasmine, don't go causing trouble, okay? That guy—Quincy, he just joined us for lunch. It has nothing to do with me," Destini told her. "Am I supposed to chase him?"

"Hey, girl," Jasmine sang, "you're getting all steamed. It's like they say—the

169

guilty don't need no accuser. You're a flirt, little sister, that's what you are."

Alonee and Sami came walking over. "What's goin' down here?" Sami asked.

"Jasmine is saying I was flirting with Quincy," Destini said. "She's trying to stir up trouble between me and Tyron."

"He stupid enough to care what this gossipy girl has to say?" Sami hissed with contempt. "Jasmine, you are one toxic sister."

Jasmine shrugged and walked away.

Alonee stared at Destini and observed her. "Destini, you are shaking like a leaf. You're scared of him, aren't you?"

"Of Tyron?" Destini said. "No I'm not. I love him and he loves me. You should see the beautiful gift he got for me. I'll show it to you guys sometime. Anyway, I better get to class. The bell is gonna ring in a minute."

Destini looked for Tyron on the football field but he'd already left. She made up her mind to find him after the last class and tell him what Jasmine was trying to do. Maybe

Jasmine had a crush on Tyron and she was trying to break up Destini and Tyron for that reason. Or maybe she was just mean.

After the final class of the day, Destini went searching for Tyron. It was getting late and she missed her bus. She would have to wait for the second one. Finally, she found him near the American history classroom. "I've been looking for you," he cried.

"I've been looking all over for you, Tyron. I missed you at lunch," Destini said.

"Didn't Jasmine come and tell you I was doing football practice?" Tyron asked.

"Yeah, she did, but not right away. I want to talk to you about that, Tyron," Destini explained. "Jasmine is a trouble-maker. She wants to make trouble for us. When I couldn't find you for lunch, I sat down with Sami and Alonee. And then this guy, Quincy Pierce, he comes along and Sami invites him to eat with us. Well, there's Jasmine spying on me and thinking

I'm friends with Quincy and I don't even know the guy. I don't know why Jasmine is doing this but—"

"She cares about me," Tyron interrupted. "She knows how much I love you and how this stuff is tearing me up."

"What stuff?" Destini demanded.

A terrible look came over Tyron's face. "The way you flirt with other guys even though you know I love you. First it was Derrick Shaw, and now this creep. I gave you that gold chain and took you to that great party. I did everything I could to prove to you how much I loved you, and still you do this to me." His voice was wavy and emotional.

"Tyron, no," Destini cried. "That's insane. I never flirted with Derrick or this guy. It's all insane."

"Just tell me the truth, Destini. It's okay. Just tell me what I gotta do to make you loyal to me," Tyron insisted. "I'll do anything."

Destini was now very frightened. She backed away from Tyron. "Tyron, I am loyal to you. I always have been. Please Tyron, calm down," she told him. She was turning to run from him when he lunged at her and grabbed her arm.

"Destini, I gave you the gold chain . . . I tried so hard . . . what's the matter with you? Why do you keep going after other guys?" Tyron demanded. He had begun to cry.

"Let me go!" Destini pleaded. "You're hurting me."

Tyron began twisting Destini's arm behind her back, and she screamed. They were near enough to the American history classroom for Ms. McDowell to hear her. The teacher was working late today.

Ms. McDowell came running from the classroom. "Let Destini go!" she yelled at Tyron as she got nearer. He ignored her. The teacher reached Destini and Tyron, stood her ground, and barked at Tyron: "*Let her go, I said!*" Tyron released

Destini, stepped back, and then fled out the door and around the back of the building.

Ms. McDowell put her arm around Destini's shoulders. "Are you okay?" she asked.

"Yeah, I'm okay . . . he almost broke my arm!" Destini whimpered.

"He's hurt you before, hasn't he?" the teacher inquired.

Destini nodded yes. "He punched me in the face and cut my lip, but he swore he'd never hurt me again."

"We have to report this to the police, Destini," Ms. McDowell advised. "This is a serious matter. Tyron is dangerous. There needs to be action taken. You understand that, don't you?"

Tears streamed down Destini's face. "I don't want him to get in trouble," she sobbed. "I still care about him. But I don't want to see him again, *not ever*."

Ms. McDowell and Mr. Hawthorne were very helpful when the police showed up. The officers took Destini's statement,

174

checked with Ms. McDowell, and assured them that the boy would be dealt with. The teacher then drove Destini home in her van.

As soon as Destini got home, she took the box containing the gold chain and pendant and mailed it to the Becker home. She destroyed the poetry page Tyron had given her. All the while she was doing this, she was sobbing. Her heart ached so much she thought something inside her would break. But nothing broke. She just continued to cry.

Destini's mother took her in her arms and rocked her back and forth as she used to do when Destini was a little girl and was sick or troubled. That helped a little.

Destini thought she would never be able to smile or laugh again. She thought she would never trust another boy. But little by little, as she became absorbed in her classes, life got a little better. Tyron Becker did not return to Tubman High. He went somewhere for anger management treatment. Destini hoped his father would get

175

help too so that Mrs. Becker would have a better life.

Several weeks after the incident with Tyron, on a Sunday night, Destini's mother got a phone call. Destini heard her talking seriously on the phone for a few minutes. Then Mom came to Destini's room. "I know you been through a lot, baby," she sighed. "These past few weeks ain't been easy for you. Last thing I want to do is add to your pain, but I just heard from your Uncle Anson. Your daddy has passed away."

Destini and her mother went to the funeral home to discuss the costs of a regular burial. Choosing the least expensive casket, having him taken to church in a simple ceremony, and then getting him buried beside his parents in Good Hope cemetery would cost $7,000. All Destini's mother had in the bank toward Destini's college expenses was $6,000. The amount wasn't going to go very far when Destini actually went off to college, but still parting with a dime of it had always broken Mom's heart.

"We've got to, Mom," Destini told her. "I don't care if I have to work like a dog all through college. He's my daddy. I want him buried in a decent way, like he was loved by somebody. I want the funeral in the church and him buried on that grass hill where Grandma and Grandpa are."

"Child, I understand," Mom said sorrowfully. "I can hardly bear to do it, but I will."

They made all the arrangements. Mom borrowed the extra thousand dollars on her credit card. Now all of Destini's college money was gone, and they were an additional thousand dollars in debt.

The following Saturday afternoon, the funeral of Arthur Fletcher was held in Pastor Bromley's church. Even though Destini's father never attended this or any church, the minister spoke kindly of him and reminded everyone of the unconditional love of God.

There were a few flowers around the casket and a single rose alongside the dead man. Destini's father wore a nice black suit that Mom had hurriedly bought at the thrift store because nothing in his closet was fit to wear at his own funeral. He looked peaceful and even happy lying there with his hands folded.

Destini was amazed and touched by how many kids and parents came from Tubman High School for the funeral. Jaris and his parents came, as well as Sami, Alonee, and Trevor and his family. Kevin came with his grandparents. Ms. McDowell came, stopping to give Destini a hug. Even Mr. Pippin came in his rumpled suit. A few of Dad's old cronies came and sat in the back. They were his drinking and gambling companions.

Finally, the service began. "We now commend our brother, Arthur Fletcher, to the Good Lord who created him," Pastor Bromley intoned. Pastor Bromley's wife, in her pleasant contralto voice, sang "The Old Rugged Cross."

The burial at Good Hope Cemetery was

CHAPTER TEN

private. Only Destini and her mother were there. It was late in the afternoon, and the grave had already been dug. The casket stood alongside it, waiting to be lowered once the last good-byes were said.

Destini placed a yellow rose atop the closed casket.

Then, as the red disc of a sun was almost down, one last mourner appeared at the cemetery. Anson Fletcher came running toward Destini and her mother, carrying a manila envelope. Anson had loved his brother, but not much. Yet years ago, Dad had given his brother a manila envelope and told him that, if anything ever happened to him, to give the envelope to Dad's widow and daughter.

"What's this, Anson?" Destini's mother asked in a weary voice as she took the sealed envelope.

"Arthur gave me this ages ago," Anson explained. "He said if he should pass, I had to make sure you get it. I had forgotten all about it. But a few hours ago I remembered it and here it is."

Mom looked at Destini. "He's probably apologizing for all he done to us," she sighed to no one in particular. "For all the years he never give me money to raise our child . . ."

Destini wept softly. She couldn't stop. She loved Daddy the best she could. When all was said and done, he was her father, and she loved him as her father. She thought about the last time she saw him alive, when he smiled and winked at her. She felt he was trying to say that he sort of loved her too. Staring at the casket, she thought, "Daddy, I loved you. If you really loved me, you never told me."

Destini's mother opened the old envelope. Her eyes went wide. "It's an insurance policy. It's a paid-up policy! He must've bought it when you were born, Destini. He was having luck with the ponies in those days . . ."

Destini said nothing. Her throat ached from crying. She looked at her mother and waited.

"Fifty thousand dollars!" Mom exclaimed. "And here's a note . . . 'Dear Sadie and Destini: I'm sorry, Daddy.'"

In the years to come, Destini would think a lot about what Tyron had done and how her daddy had lived his life. And maybe someday she would be able to sort out the reasons for their behavior. For now, she was content to believe that her father told her that he really loved her.

Destini fell into her mother's arms, and they both stood there together, crying until the sun went down.